VISIONARY TRIBUTES

"The resonance I feel with Damanhur and the mission of The Oracle Institute fills me with passionate promise for the future of the human race. Coherence of this magnitude is a clear indication of a deep pattern within the universe, and it is the same force which guides my work at the Foundation for Conscious Evolution, The Shift Network, and with colleagues throughout the world."

~ **Barbara Marx Hubbard,** co-founder of the Foundation for Conscious Evolution; global ambassador for The Shift Network; member of the Evolutionary Leaders Group, World Future Society, and Assoc. for Global New Thought; and author of *The Hunger of Eve, Emergence: The Shift from Ego to Essence,* and *Birth 2012 and Beyond*

"The Damanhur community is a truly paradigm-expanding experiment in conscious living. Its design, evolution, and artistry are a testament to the unique genius of Falco – an evolutionary pioneer."

~ **Stephen Dinan, M.A.,** founder and CEO of The Shift Network; member of the Evolutionary Leaders Group; and author of *Radical Shift: Spiritual Writings from the Voices of Tomorrow* and *Sacred America: Fulfilling Our Country's Promise* with Marianne Williamson

"Here is the revelation of the soul of a mystery school, that once and future experience of exploring the ways in which the self is put into service for the SELF ... and the world mind grows as a consequence."

~ **Jean Houston, Ph.D.,** founder of The Foundation for Mind Research, Renaissance of Spirit Mystery School, and the Jean Houston Foundation for social artistry; global advisor on human development to the United Nations and UNICEF; and author of *A Passion for the Possible, A Mythic Life,* and *The Wizard of Us*

"These books are a poetic tribute to the Absolute bearing witness to its own creation through the eyes of a deeply inspired mystic."

~ **Andrew Cohen,** spiritual teacher and founder of EnlightenNext; and author of *My Master Is My Self, Embracing Heaven & Earth,* and *Evolutionary Enlightenment* with Deepak Chopra

"History hinges on the lives and actions of great individuals. Building the Temples of Humankind was a mission from a higher spiritual world. Falco has inspired a community to bring heaven to earth."

> ~ **Alex Grey and Allyson Grey, M.F.A,** founders of the Chapel of Sacred Mirrors (CoSM), a sanctuary for encouraging the creative spirit; publishers of *Damanhur: Temples of Humankind;* and Alex is Chair of the Sacred Art Department at Wisdom University and author of *Sacred Mirrors, The Mission of Art,* and *Net of Being*

"Falco is an explorer at the frontiers of the human experience. He sees what others only intuit, and he thereby provides insight into the potential for the human future in that domain of our identity where there are at present deep yearnings but no maps."

> ~ **Jim Garrison, Ph.D.,** founder and CEO of Ubiquity University; founder of Wisdom University and The State of the World Forum; and author of *America As Empire, Civilization and The Transformation of Power,* and *Climate Change and the Primordial Mind*

"This look into the personal perspectives of Falco – a living Avatar – is a poetic walk through the internal work and wisdom of one who has brought us astonishing beauty and creativity. You'll find practical wisdom interwoven with cosmic musings that result in a provocative and enlightening window into the mind of a very special man."

> ~ **John L. Petersen,** futurist and founder of The Arlington Institute; author of *A Vision for 2012: Planning for Extraordinary Change* and *Out of the Blue: How to Anticipate Big Future Surprises;* and publisher of the e-newsletter *FUTUREdition*

"The *Three Books of the Initiate* are uniquely different than any other spiritual books on the market today – and I do mean unique. They read as if Oberto were interpreting my third near-death experience, seeing what I saw, feeling what I felt, lending heft to that sense of Presence when you truly become one with The One. The texts stretch thought about who we are, where we came from, and why we're here. The books are stunningly powerful."

> ~ **P.M.H. Atwater, L.H.D.,** researcher of near-death and evolutionary states; and author of *The Real Truth About Death, Children of the Fifth World, Beyond the Indigo Children, Future Memory,* and *Near-Death Experiences: The Rest of the Story*

"What appeals to me about Falco's exposition is that the perspective on learning and growing into the light is one of personal responsibility, with apparently no absolutes. Like Edgar Cayce's practical philosophy, it assumes each person is capable of achieving self-realization. Thanks for making this book available in English."

> ~ **Henry Reed, Ph.D.,** Director of the Edgar Cayce Institute for Intuitive Studies; professor at Atlantic University; founder of Creative Spirit Studios; and author of *Dream Medicine*, *Dream Solutions*, *Awakening Your Psychic Powers*, and *Sharing Your Intuitive Heart*

"The *Three Books of the Initiate* are a love poem to humanity, written by a man drunk with the Divine. They are a wakeup call, inviting each of us to let go of what is no longer serving us and to learn how to behave. They are an invitation to embrace the Source that is manifesting through each of us and everything, and that is patiently waiting for us to remember who we truly are."

> ~ **Philip Hellmich,** Director of Peace at The Shift Network; advisor to the Global Peace Initiative of Women; co-author of *The Love: Of the Fifth Spiritual Paradigm* (Oracle Institute Press); and author of *God and Conflict* with Lama Surya Das

"Reading Falco's inspiring books feels like dancing with the Divine. The ego wants to find the logic, but through story and metaphor, the jewels of wisdom land deeply within the soul, resulting in profoundly effortless understanding and illumination."

> ~ **Olivia Parr-Rud, M.S.,** thought-leader and liaison between the spiritual and corporate worlds; and best-selling author of *Data Mining Cookbook* and *Business Intelligence Success Factors: Tools for Aligning Your Business in the Global Economy*

"The *Initiate* series reads like an epic poem. The nature of the Cosmos unfolds throughout these passages, along with the truth of the divine relationship between God and the creatures of Earth. For those who are ready to hear, many mysteries are revealed through the Master's midnight conversations, his secret thoughts, and his guiding hand offered to the Initiates."

> ~ **High Malku Priest Robert Martin, Jr., Ph.D.,** Patriarch of the Ancient and Sovereign Order of Melchizedek; and author of *The Tree of Life Bears Twelve Manner of Fruit: An Alchemical Story*

SEVEN SCARLET DOORS

Third Book of the Initiate

OBERTO *"Falco"* AIRAUDI

WITH A FOREWORD BY
BARBARA MARX HUBBARD

Translated by Elaine Baxendale and
Silvia "Esperide Ananas" Buffagni
Edited by Laura M. George

Published by The Oracle Institute Press, LLC

A division of The Oracle Institute, a 501(c)(3) educational charity
1990 Battlefield Drive
Independence, Virginia 24348
www.TheOracleInstitute.org

Copyright © 2013 by Oberto Airaudi

Revised English Edition

Publisher's Cataloging-in-Publication Data

Airaudi, Oberto.
    Seven scarlet doors / Oberto "Falco" Airaudi ; with a foreword by Barbara Marx Hubbard ; translated by Elaine Baxendale and Silvia "Esperide Ananas" Buffagni ; edited by Laura M. George. -- Rev. English ed.
    p. cm. -- (Third book of the Initiate)
    LCCN 2013934831
    ISBN 978-1-937465-09-4

    1. End of the world--Fiction. 2. Messiah--Fiction.
3. Human-alien encounters--Fiction. 4. Science fiction.
I. Baxendale, Elaine. II. Ananas, Esperide.
III. Title. IV. Series: Airaudi, Oberto. Initiate ; 3rd bk.

PS3601.I78S48 2013   813'.6
                                              QBI13-677

Cover and book design by Donna Montgomery
Printed in the United States

CONTENTS

PUBLISHER'S NOTE

Seven Scarlet Doors is the final book in the *Initiate* series written by Oberto "Falco" Airaudi. It is a stand-alone work; however the prequel – *Road to the Central Fires* – provides additional instructions and clues that some Initiates may find helpful in decoding the trilogy, which includes: *Dying to Learn: First Book of the Initiate* and *Reborn to Live: Second Book of the Initiate.*

Altogether, the *Initiate* texts explain the "Game of Life," which is a term Falco uses for the Forces which impact our planet and the evolutionary trajectory of humanity.

Road to the Central Fires is available at the Oracle website as a free e-book to complement the last installment of the trilogy. It describes eight rooms or dreams that set forth principal steps toward inner-alchemy and enlightenment, as taught at the Damanhur Mystery School. The prequel tells of one night around a campfire, spent at the side of Vadusfadam, the Monk who has come to Earth after a great cataclysm to assist with our spiritual awakening. Vadusfadam was the pupil of Master OroCritshna, whom we met in the first book, *Dying to Learn.* In the second book, *Reborn to Live*, a new crop of Initiates follows Vadusfadam, who continues the great work of preparing them (and you) for the New Era.

Take care, Reader: *No word herein is written by chance.* Also pay attention to colors, directions, and passages that prompt your deep recognition and memory.

And here is a preliminary clue: *This text is linked to the mystery of Enkidu and the number 8.*

FOREWORD
Barbara Marx Hubbard

Planet Earth is a living organism. It has hit a set of global crises that could lead to the destruction of our life support system ... and at the very same moment, we see the glimmers of an emerging cocreative culture. This culture is arising through the lives of a new generation of pioneering souls who are awakened from within by the Impulse of Evolution, connected through the heart to the whole of life, and attuned to the patterns of creation. Humanity is gaining cosmic consciousness and developing powers we used to attribute to our gods.

This new humanity is carrying the seed of a cocreative society, a synergistic democracy, the next stage of human evolution. We are facing the crisis of the birth of a universal humanity capable of coevolving with nature and cocreating with Spirit.

We are all members of ONE generation. No one on earth is living on the other side of this crisis to tell us what to do. Yet there are some who are guiding us through this unprecedented shift toward this new era of evolution: *evolution by choice, not chance.*

Oberto "Falco" Airaudi, founder and spiritual guide for The Federation of Damanhur, is such a universal human.

The Wheel of Cocreation

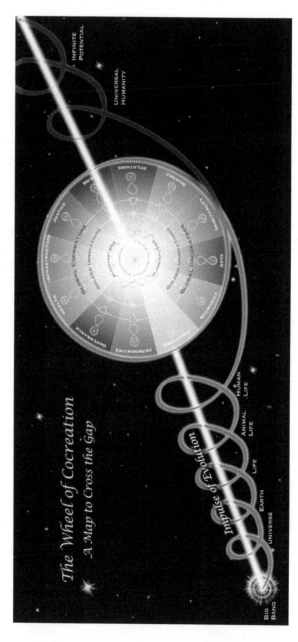

He has incarnated at precisely this moment in planetary history to signal to members of the human species what they can become. He is a true Avatar with total recollection of prior lives and his current life mission. He has been cocreating with the Divine, or the pattern in the Process of Creation, the Consciousness Force for the past half-century.

Starting in 1975, Falco began building Damanhur with a core group of other committed souls. They chose an isolated town at the base of the Italian Alps to manifest their dream: *the first full spectrum, sustainable, spiritual community on planet Earth.*

During this same period of time, I began to envision a model for a whole system shift on planet Earth. It came to me as the Wheel of Cocreation, which is a graphic representation of a full spectrum community. The Wheel is our turn on the spiral of evolution.

At the hub of the Wheel is Spirit – the Evolutionary Impulse – coming through us collectively. It is a new sacred space, where through resonance and revelation, we pick up the patterns of evolution and are guided toward our own calling within the emerging whole system. The hub is surrounded by a Communion of Pioneering Souls, our non-local contact with the vast and rising community of cocreators throughout the earth and beyond. Then comes the ring called Planetary DNA. It symbolizes our discovery of the patterns of our evolution emerging as a natural design or structure of the whole organic body of planet Earth. This DNA is best discovered by identifying projects – Golden Innovations – that work in every sector of the Wheel and that demonstrate the actuality of a sustainable, evolvable world.

When we initiate a process of synergistic convergence within the Wheel of Cocreation, we invite groups in each sector to seek common goals and match needs with resources in light of the capacities of the entire system. This process is called "SYNergistic CONvergence" (SYNCON), and it was developed and tested in the 1970s by my Committee for the Future in Washington, D.C., and in many town meetings since then. The process results in social synergy, the coming together of separate parts to form a new whole, greater than and different from the sum of its parts. SYNCON is an experience of social love that inspires attraction.

I believe these efforts are the early phases of a more synergistic democracy where each person is free to do and be their best. Thus, Thomas Jefferson's great statement, "All men are created equal," is now expanded to affirm: *We hold these truths to be self evident; all people are born creative …*

Today the Foundation for Conscious Evolution, which I co-founded in 1990, is bringing forth the Wheel of Cocreation as a model for community-based "Synergy Hubs." These Hubs are invited to form themselves as microcosms of the whole system in their communities, communicating what is working locally, connecting with one another globally, and together forming seeds of the new cocreative culture. These regional Synergy Hubs will work together toward the formation of a Global Wheel of Cocreation, filled with projects that work. The Global Wheel will scan for, map, connect and communicate what is working throughout the world. We envision a magnificent "unveiling" of humanity's creative potential. All of this is featured in my book *Birth 2012 and Beyond: Humanity's Great Shift to the Age of Conscious Evolution.*

It is for this vision that my name was placed in nomination for Vice President of the United States on the

Democratic ticket in 1984, when I proposed that an "Office for the Future" and a "Peace Room" as sophisticated as a war room be developed in the office of the vice presidency. My speech at the 1984 Democratic National Convention is on YouTube: http://www.youtube.com/watch?v=D1FWXm-8FGs.

All these activities are natural expressions of a "post-birth" humanity, post the December 22, 2012 "announcement" of the new era of our evolution which I co-produced with The Shift Network. Today, many groups are working together to cultivate the emerging cocreative society, and our planetary organism is now seeding itself with social organs that can grow and sustain an ever-evolving world.

Thus, although we lived on opposite ends of the earth and had never met, Falco and I were cocreating the same vision in the 1970s, with the cosmos and with each other.

My mystical connection to Damanhur also happens to coincide with recent scientific discoveries: (i) the "field" and "entanglement" in quantum physics; (ii) "strange attractors" in chaos theory; and (iii) "zero point energy" and Higgs boson in particle physics. Teilhard de Chardin, a Catholic priest and mystic, credited these unseen energies to God – *the Alpha and the Omega.* And he used the term "Omega Point" to describe the evolutionary (heavenly) impulse that nourishes us during the confusion of ever-increasing complexity, and then directs us toward a shared higher consciousness.

At the Foundation for Conscious Evolution, we believe the Wheel of Cocreation provides a comprehensive yet simple template of 21st Century living. Moreover, we assert that the Wheel will assist in expanding the global coherence that was felt around the world on our collective birthday: December 22, 2012.

The Wheel of Cocreation

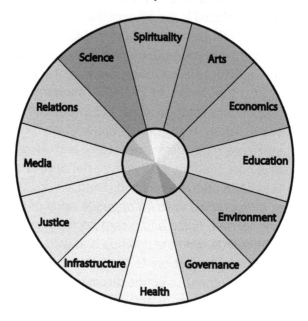

To prove my point, let's take a moment to look at the twelve delineated sectors. Then, let's compare the sectors to the Damanhur experience to determine whether Falco intuitively used the Wheel to build the "most utopian community on the planet," the praise accorded by numerous social scientists, philosophers, historians, and futurists.

The Twelve Sectors of a Full Spectrum Community

1. **Arts:** Music, fine arts, crafts, performing arts. The realm of creative expression through various media.
2. **Economics:** From gifting to high finance, the micro to the macro, including all forms of currency and financial markets, both formal and informal, local to global.

3. **Education:** Formal and informal, for all ages, species and cross-species. Awareness of cultural memes and assumptions, perceptual filters, scientific studies, the brain while learning, and the psychology of learning.

4. **Environment:** In its broadest sense, the environment is the context in which all else takes place within the complex adaptive systems of earth. Everything within the environment is connected to and affected by human design (or lack thereof).

5. **Governance:** Our governmental designs reveal who and what we value. In the future, the purpose and structure of this sector will reflect the diversity of human and life systems and reach beyond mere organizational design to embrace all scales, from self-governance to entire nations, from classroom to boardroom, and from human society to natural systems.

6. **Health:** Concepts of health have evolved with our awareness, making this one of the most dynamically shifting areas of human understanding. What happens inside our bodies is directly affected by what happens around us. We are not separate beings, but complex adaptive systems-within-systems. We are only beginning to explore whole-systems and perception itself.

7. **Infrastructure:** Though most consider infrastructure the basic underlying framework of a system within the confines of human design, it can apply to any internal framework or systems organization. Traditionally, it refers to facilities and systems that serve a given locale: transportation, energy, communication systems, schools, military, food systems, etc. Once again, the structure of the design determines its outcome.

8. **Justice:** Justice systems reflect our sense of equity, morals, and values. Our awareness of the complexity of life has evolved along with our ability to handle those complexities, and that has forced us to reevaluate our sense of justice over time, our understanding of context and relativity, and our ability to perceive truth and fairness in any given situation – both individually and collectively – moving toward a more restorative justice.

9. **Media:** Any means of communication is technically part of the media, but what that encompasses keeps growing, and along with it, the breadth of its power to influence. The difference between reflecting what is and creating it has blurred, as well as the ethics regarding use, structure, and content. How can we develop a planetary nervous system sensitive to the "new" news of what is working to produce a more sustainable, creative and loving world?

10. **Relations:** In the past, relationships were thought of as human-to-human. But with the advent of whole-systems thinking and perceiving, our attention has shifted beyond the mere elements of any given system (e.g.: economic, natural), to the relationships among those elements. For example, our understanding of communication itself, including the impact of conflict or active listening skills on communication, has expanded tremendously, opening the door to a new era of relational intimacy across all scales, individual to global.

11. **Science:** Instead of viewing this sector as being comprised of separate fields, imagine innovations in biology, information science, physical and space sciences, and the psychologies of transformation all merging and cross-pollinating with each other. Interdisciplinary science is now allowing for greater insights and awareness of the interdependence of all sectors, systems, and life itself.

12. **Spirituality:** Throughout history, spirituality has always referred to the incorporeal aspects, the intangible underlying patterns that humans perceive in the meta-vision of life itself. The Wheel of Cocreation invites us to place that seeming invisible thread of Evolutionary Impulse at the center of our human systems designs and consciously create *with* instead of in dominance *over* nature's systems, understanding that there is no separation between the two. There is a progressive direction and spirit-action within evolution, leading toward systems of higher complexity, greater consciousness, and more synergistic order.

Damanhur's art, including stained-glass, mosaics, and jewelry, is prized throughout the world. Citizens showcase their art at a central gallery, Damanhur Crea, and they perform musical, dance, and theatrical productions on a variety of inside stages and outdoor amphitheaters.

Residents live in "nuclei" (i.e., neighborhoods), which are optimally populated at roughly 20 people. The group homes and apartments are energy efficient and cooperatively managed. Others live on farms, where they grow the food, make olive oil, and tend livestock. The community is mostly self-sustainable, utilizing forestry practices, hydro electricity, solar energy, and internal food production and water conservation.

The citizens operate dozens of regional and virtual businesses. The micro-economy also boasts the Damanhur "Credito," which is a complementary currency tied to the Euro. Their businesses primarily use the cooperative form of ownership (i.e., employee owned). Other sectors – such as communications and media, science and technology, and infrastructure – are profit centers for the Federation.

Health care, you may ask? They've got that covered too, with outpatient facilities and use of natural medicines. They also internally handle conflict (which is rare) and security, which mainly focuses on the free flow of Damanhur visitors, who are always welcome, and Damanhur vehicles, which are communally shared.

The community also has its own elementary and secondary schools where the children are exposed to travel, allowed to experiment, and encouraged to ultimately identify their personal life paths and careers.

So let's see: *Where are we on the Wheel of Cocreation?* It seems that Damanhur has every sector covered so far with just two remaining: governance and spirituality (a/k/a politics and religion). How does Damanhur handle these challenging topics when liberal democracies based on opposition and win-lose voting are failing us everywhere?

As of this writing, Damanhur is being governed pursuant to its tenth Constitution ... but blink and they may adopt an eleventh. Damanhurians are not afraid of debate, admitting they've hit a road block, or changing course. And they periodically review their "laws" to evaluate whether community needs are being met. If not, then it's time to rewrite the community rules. Incidentally, the Federation is managed by three elected "Guides," none of whom is Falco.

Finally we arrive at the spirituality sector, home of my heart. Depending on how you perceive the Wheel, this sector is either the first or the twelfth – *Alpha and Omega!* Consequently, this is the sector that binds all communities. It also is the sector through which we may objectively assess a community's true nature. So how, exactly, do Damanhurians express, share, and celebrate their spirituality?

To begin with, every adult pursues a path of spiritual inquiry and practice that is freely chosen. Additionally, Damanhur has a Mystery School, for which Falco wrote the *Three Books of the Initiate*. Students also study ancient hermetic principles, proven theosophies, even astral travel. The curriculum's objectives include the quest for truth, inner alchemy, transcendence, and enlightenment.

Then there are the Temples to Humanity, which are built on underground energy points called "Synchronic Lines." Truly astounding, the Temples are called the "Eighth Wonder of the World," due to the intricacy and inclusiveness of the many sacred spaces. Starting with ancient Goddess worship, every belief system is honored. Hence, the underlying message of this underground complex is that we have gradually evolved from being God's children to God's partners, in full unity with and supported by Divine Forces.

However, in the *Initiate* series Falco speaks not only about the "Divine Forces." He also writes about the "Enemy of Humankind" or the "Dark Forces." Be forewarned, there is no New Age jargon in these books. Rather, Falco delivers hard punches, openly acknowledging the duality of the earth plane and the anti-evolutionary energies that try to thwart our collective progress. That is how the trilogy starts, in fact, with a great cataclysm that leaves us shattered.

Ervin Laszlo, renowned professor of systems science, futurist, and mutual friend of mine and Falco's, has coined the term "Chaos Point" to refer to the period of dramatic tension that occurs when a system is suffering severe disequilibrium. At such times, a wide range of assailants attack the system. Case in point, our current challenges: global warming, desertification, water shortages, famine, disease, economic disparity, greed, corruption, hopelessness, terrorism, war ...

In *Birth 2012 and Beyond*, Dr. Laszlo explains that initially a system will attempt to self-correct by relying on old solutions. However, if the system is stressed to the breaking point due to multiple novel and unanticipated challenges, then it faces an unprecedented test. In such a situation, regression as a form of problem solving will not work. Instead, the system must eliminate the disorder by working through it, transcending it, finding higher order and new structure ... or else the system will crash.

> *We have reached a watershed in our societal evolution. The science of systems tells us that when complex open systems – such as living organisms, and also ecologies and societies of organisms – approach a condition of critical instability, they face a moment of truth: they either transform or break down. Humankind is approaching that moment of truth: a global bifurcation.*

The bifurcation to which Dr. Laszlo refers is the same choice that Time Monk Vadusfadam presents to the Initiates (and the reader) in *Seven Scarlet Doors:* Specifically, will we commit to the search for enlightenment, not just for our own edification, but for the survival of our species?

I agree that humans are the first species to *consciously* face extinction by our own acts. And I agree that there are both evolutionary and anti-evolutionary forces at play. The "Game of Life," as Falco calls it, is real, as is the "Cosmic Code" described by James Gardner in his book *The Intelligent Universe:*

> The universe is coming to life, purposely and in accordance with a finely tuned cosmic code that is the precise functional equivalent of DNA in the terrestrial biosphere. … [It] furnishes a recipe for the self-assembly of offspring.

Truly, we hold the fate of our world in our own hands. I believe that the world participation on December 22, 2012, announcing the birth of a new era, had an effect on all who participated. It infused the "noosphere" – the global brain/mind – with heart, love, and creativity. It affected the nervous system of the world. Ever more of us recognize that we are personally being born into the next phase of our evolution.

I believe that we are up to the task. In fact we were born for it. As a mother and a grandmother, I know how terrifying and dangerous childbirth can be. Yet, the process is natural and we feel an unconditional love for the unknown child.

From an evolutionary perspective, witnessing nature's rise over billions of years from no-thing at all to every-thing, we gain the perspective of radical optimism. Nature "optimizes." It creates ever greater whole systems out of separate parts. We see ourselves as part of the natural trauma of birth, overgrowing the womb of earth, being pressured by the life force itself to evolve to survive.

This is the greatest wakeup call the human species has ever faced. My sense is that universal, cocreative, evolving humans are arising everywhere and that together we possess the wisdom to birth the New Era.

Currently, Damanhur is the only "City of Light" on earth. No other community has propagated as many sectors on the Wheel of Cocreation. Privately, Falco says that we must quickly manifest Cities of Light all around the globe, or else we will not survive this critical juncture in human history. This is why I am promoting Synergy Hubs and Shift Circles, to bring leadership and hope to the uninitiated.

I am very excited to hear that Falco's publisher – The Oracle Institute – is facilitating a Shift Circle and using the Wheel of Cocreation to manifest a full spectrum community along the New River in Independence, Virginia. Following Damanhur's example, Oracle is anchoring its "Valley of Light" project by first building sacred space: the "Peace Pentagon." This center will operate as an interfaith sanctuary, retreat, and social justice think tank. I trust that Oracle will succeed in building the Valley of Light in the New River Valley. Where better for New Humans to build the New World?

The resonance I feel with Damanhur and the mission of The Oracle Institute fills me with passionate promise for the future of the human race. For me, coherence of this magnitude is a clear indication of a deep pattern within the universe, and it is the same force which guides my work at the Foundation for Conscious Evolution, The Shift Network, and with colleagues throughout the world.

In closing, allow me to underscore the poignant and prescient manner by which Falco commences this last installment of the *Initiate* trilogy. In his Preamble, Falco gently queries: "*Perhaps this is the era of WOMEN.*"

I believe this is true! Right-brained, feminine wisdom holds the key to unlocking and building the New Era. When Oracle founder Laura George approached me to do the Foreword to *Seven Scarlet Doors*, she highlighted the importance of having a woman introduce the last book. She too understands that the Godhead has been out of balance, serving only to increase the level of dysfunction on earth. Our institutions – political, ecclesiastical, and governmental – are all woefully overweighed in left-brain masculine energy. There simply is no positive way forward until the "can-do" impulse is properly matched with the "should-do" impetus. In short, love and cocreation, masculine and feminine joined is the answer to every question in the New Era.

My good friend Jean Houston sums it up this way, in her essay entitled "Living on the Eve of the New Story," which appears in *Birth 2012 and Beyond:*

> *Critical to this reformation is a true partnership society, in which women join men in the full social agenda. Since women tend to emphasize process over product – "being" rather than "doing," "deepening" rather than "end-goaling" – it is inevitable that as a result of this partnership, our current reliance on linear, sequential solutions will yield to a way of knowing that comes from seeing things in whole constella- tions rather than as discrete facts.*

Certainly, Falco is one man who has demonstrated the great work as a symbol. It is truly an honor and privilege to write this introduction to the magnificent work of Falco. I am looking forward to our first meeting. What a joy that will be. And who can predict what will happen!

Barbara Marx Hubbard

Barbara Marx Hubbard has been called "the voice for conscious evolution of our time" by Deepak Chopra, and she is the subject of Neale Donald Walsch's new book, *The Mother of Invention.* A prolific author, visionary, social innovator, evolutionary thinker and educator, she is co-founder and president of the Foundation for Conscious Evolution. She also is the producer and narrator of the award-winning documentary series entitled *Humanity Ascending: A New Way through Together.*

Recently, Barbara has partnered with The Shift Network as a global ambassador for the conscious evolution movement: a shift from evolution by *chance* toward evolution by *choice*. Along with Shift, she launched the "Agents of Conscious Evolution" training and formed an international team to co-produce a global multi-media event on December 22, 2012 entitled "Birth 2012: Cocreating a Planetary Shift in Time," an historic, turning-point event designed to awaken the social, spiritual, scientific, and technological potential of humanity.

In 1984, Barbara's name was placed in nomination for the Vice Presidency of the United States on the Democratic ticket. She called for a "Peace Room" to scan for, map, connect, and communicate what is working in America and throughout the world. Barbara also co-chaired Soviet-American Citizen Summits, introducing a new concept called SYNCON to foster synergistic convergence with opposing groups.

Barbara has established a Chair in Conscious Evolution at Wisdom University, and she is a member of many progressive organizations, including Evolutionary Leaders Group, Transformational Leadership Council, Association for Global New Thought (AGNT), and The World Future Society.

www.Evolve.org

PREAMBLE
The Era of Women

Perhaps this is the era of WOMEN. Of their liberation, of their growing beyond men.

Intuition – the feminine side of each one of us, the feminine mystery of ourselves – will be revealed to us soon. The great value of silence and that which is veiled discovered.

The women travelling with the Time Monk Vadusfadam are extraordinary. Perhaps they will have an advantage in dreaming the answers to the Seven Scarlet Doors. Already, they wear a veil of awareness, and the mystery that emanates from it gives them power.

Has the new woman already been born?
She who knows how to be romantic, gentle, ambitious, courageous, maternal, determined. She who will be all those things in the same order, at the same time?

What woman will take her seat upon the mirror of this island of the world? Surasundari – the messenger, vessel, vestal, Lady of the Forces – who she knows to be within her?[1]

Vadusfadam talks of Cybele: the Divine Mother, chthonic, generator of the Four Elements, Lady of the Lions, she who is worshipped in the black stone.[2]
To her, the Time Monk has dedicated the drums that perhaps one day you will play.
Great Mother of the Gods and Humankind, element of Union, and protector in the search for the Divine ... how many things have been said about this Goddess of whom you likely know nothing!

Will there grow a female race that will be able to read every mystery, that knows contemplation because they know how to push beyond their own apparent strength?
Will there be Ladies of the Moon and Sun, Mothers and Daughters of the Central Fire?

These and more are the questions posed by the Monk Vadusfadam to his Initiates. He wants them to think about female wisdom, about the ideals which purify, about that stellar charm which can rise in this half of Humankind.
And he traces this drawing, saying that by its means we enter into the heart of the Feminine Force.

---

[1] Surasundari is a Hindu goddess symbolizing enchanted beauty.
[2] Cybele is an Anatolian mother goddess, who dates to 6,000 B.C.E. She was later adopted in Greek mythology. She is the "Great Mother."

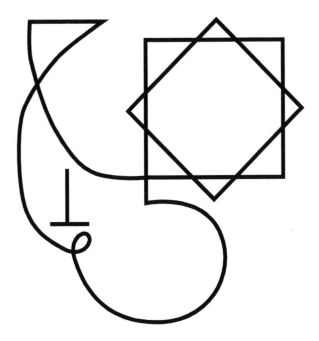

The second road to the Central Fires will be difficult, and the pale moon seems to be turned the wrong way, rolling over many times in the sky.

At times the moon has a pleasing voice; at times she is a mere detail enlarged in the mind.

Lady of the Moon, awaken thyself.

Awaken within the Initiates, within everyone, within YOU!

Part One
The First Scarlet Door

This is the question we are all thinking: "Where are you taking us, Master?" We are following a path that does not exist yet. We are walking in empty space to go where?

Where mountains are born? Where life is more comprehensible? Where Humankind never heard of original sin?

Vadusfadam replies, "This is the second road, the one that always leads to the Central Fires. The first encampment is behind us. Now I will lead you, if you want, to RED."

I want to recount his exact words as faithfully as possible. *What does it mean to be "led to RED"?*

We are high up in the mountains, but we can breathe. For hours we have been walking along terrifying escarpments. A pale moon has risen in spite of the diffused light.

We are crazy wanderers, that much is certain. We are leaving behind the security of the nothing we used to own in exchange for the uncertainty of the infinite.

The burden each one of us carries is undoubtedly different: Some need to have many things with them; some don't feel the need of anything.

A pack of dogs appears to be following us. We can hear them bark louder and louder. We ask the Monk to walk faster so we can find a shelter safe from the beasts. He does not speed up. On the contrary, Vadusfadam seems to slow down a little every time one of us makes the suggestion.

Many of us are worried, afraid. Vadusfadam has a stick in his hand, which appears to give him confidence.

But there are Initiates for whom wild animals are a weak point. Driven by fear, they run ahead, leaving us behind within a few minutes.

Now, we very clearly can hear a howling cry, as wolves set upon our tracks. Where are we? Around us I can see only sharp spears of rock and sparse shoots of yellowish grass constantly shaken by a freezing wind.

I shiver. Why don't I run ahead too? I truly don't know. I know only that we are gathering tightly around the Monk.

He tells us not to turn around, but to continue walking calmly at a regular pace if we don't want to get too tired. It seems he is underestimating the danger, which is so obvious to us. Yet, we trust him and make an enormous effort not to turn around.

The pack of beasts – large in number I would say judging by their howling – is now at our backs. I tremble and feel my throat go dry, tongue stuck to the roof of my mouth. Here they come ... they have caught up with us!

The wolves stop and sniff us, snarling at some of us. They wag their tails like puppies at Vadusfadam, who seems to be whispering something to each one of them. He recommends that we remain calm and think of the wolves as affectionate dogs, imagine them as pets we had around us when we were children. Certainly, this is not easy to envision, given the circumstances.

Look, now they are starting to run fast again, ahead of us. Their howling is lost little by little, in the distance.

Time passes. The light is always the same, that of a long dawn. Then at last, we can see far ahead some of our companions who had fled. Some of them have managed to climb a solitary tree. Others, less fortunate, have been devoured by the beasts.

One Initiate, wounded, is losing a lot of blood. A bright red blood: throbbing, warm, dense with the life that is fading. The Time Monk puts his hands on the wounded man; he doesn't bother to look at the dead.

Vadusfadam will allow us to bandage the man only after lengthy questioning. Why does the Monk behave this way? I no longer recognize him. He seemed so understanding, so good to us, full of promises. Now he is unmoved by our companions who have been torn apart. He interrogates rather than heals the wounded man. I must admit that all of this makes me feel uncomfortable. I really thought he was different, a Master.

At the foot of the tree, I can see something sparkle: When one of our dead companions has been moved, a half buried crown appears.

Vadusfadam doesn't waste a glance at the dead, but with a swift gesture he picks up the jeweled object, rubs the blood off it with his sleeve, and puts it on his head for a moment. He smiles, as if he were far from the sad scene around us.

"They fled," he said. "And in so doing, they became makers of their own destiny – a destiny they were not able to guide yet. They sinned of presumption. They were already dead when they began to run, leaving us behind. Why have pity on their fate? They chose and they made a mistake."

"But they ventured out on the path to the Central Fires; they were with us," I'm thinking. I cannot understand, and the same for many of my companions. We are following Vadusfadam, but he is so different than us. He is distant, alone. It is as though we no longer can discern the humanity which so distinguished him.

He sits down and talks to us. He tells us that in following him, we have made a critical choice. Even if for some it was an emotional decision dictated by the wildest of reasons, we now have started a journey on the road which leads to RED.

The first red we already have found: the blood of our companions who fled. And he reminds us that he did not call us. Rather, it was we who followed him on this road. Whether we have been courageous, or presumptuous, is something we are bound to find out, sooner or later.

"This," he concludes, "is only the beginning."

And we realize from what has happened and from the Monk's words that this is not just an amusing game, but a profound choice that we have made. Willingly or unwillingly, we made a decision that will affect the whole of our lives.

Vadusfadam is less surly now. He invites us to reconsider our decision, and to turn around before it is too late. He says he is willing to show us the way back, and to pretend nothing has happened.

We look around at each other; a glance is sufficient. We think about it. Nobody wants to change their mind now.

He has us join hands, including the wounded man. Vadusfadam leans over the injured Initiate and blows gently on the back of his neck. We will discover before long that his wounds are healed. He is weak but already able to walk.

We set off again before dawn comes to an end.

We are walking briskly without any hitches, while the view never seems to change. Some, weighed down by too much baggage, begin to feel tired, and they ponder whether everything they have brought along is really necessary.

Now the road is rising toward a mountain pass. Little by little, the mountains fade into the distance, disappearing into the fine mist we are piercing as we walk. A sprinkling of snow makes the landscape really sharp.

Black and white, absolute patches.

The summit of the pass is closer now, and we notice above it a tall slim needle of rock leaning slightly. The light around it is brighter, while the high mountain peaks are now buried in fog so thick that it wraps around our feet.

Vadusfadam halts in the shadow of the tall, motionless, imposing rock. He bows toward it slightly and calls it, as if it were a person. We are all around him and the rock.

As we look closely at the rock, it seems to be crowned, but the Monk says we have to place on its summit the crown we found by our dead companion and the only tree we came across along this road.

Not without some effort, we set about doing it, some clambering up helped along by the others. Soon we achieved what was asked of us.

Without saying a word, our faces pointed upward, we stare in silence at our work. It is at this moment that a bright ray of sunshine breaks through and we can see a star.

The light seems to rain down upon us in a prism of colors from the crown. We are all moved, even if we can only guess why. Something escapes us, a sense of *deja vu*, a feeling that prickles the back of our necks.

Seeing our tiredness, Vadusfadam allows us to stop for a little while. We sit down next to a bush, the only one we notice in the area, a bright green and strong bush.

This is when the Time Monk talks to us of our duties, of the behavior we must adopt if we are to stay with him. He asks us to be attentive and aware in all our actions. He talks to us as one would talk to small children, but it does not offend us in the least. We all acknowledge him as our guide, the one who possesses the Force but also knows how to forgive.

In the meantime, our wounded companion has completely recovered. He even marches a little bit ahead of us along the road.

Now we pay a little more attention to each other. We organize ourselves. Still marching on, we give ourselves precise tasks: Someone will take care of cooking; someone will see to defense; someone will get the shelters ready for the night.

It is not the first time we are together, following Vadusfadam, but no other journey can be compared to this. As we discuss how to organize ourselves, my mind wanders back to the first experiences with my companions ...

Men and women of all ages, talking among ourselves, we began to get to know one another, and our imagination about each other was stirred, little by little. We cared about one another, our common journey united us. We promised to help each other, in every way, in order to be ready for anything.

Some fell in love. In the beginning, our witty jokes provoked smiles, but at times some took them a little too seriously. We saw that even those who joke were not immune to this subtle fire. Some were even jealous of the happiness of others.

Is this a grave sin? Perhaps you think you are immune, that you can only fall in love if you allow yourself to ... but are you really sure?

We were afraid for some of those in love. They distanced themselves in their thoughts from our as yet mysterious task. On several occasions some of us had to run after them, because while looking at each other and not paying sufficient attention to the road, they risked getting lost or falling down.

I noticed then how this inclination to fall in love was strange: For many it happened all of a sudden, and it reminded me more of a test than something natural. But what is natural? And should you look for it or resist it? Enjoy it, ignore it, go after it, think about it?

On the other hand, some couples knew how to distinguish between their love for each other and the aims we are pursuing on our path. Consequently, they had two pairs of eyes and two pairs of ears to grasp everybody's state of mind, the excessive jealousies, sadness and euphoria.

There were even some who left us, convinced they had found what they were looking for in their soul mate. We never heard anything more of them.

Thus, falling in love can give you new energy and more awareness, or you can lose yourself in it. This is something that is always good to bear in mind.

Vadusfadam is smiling, as we slowly descend into a wide valley. However it is still very far away and we can't carry on any more due to a sudden weariness.

Is it our emotions that make us feel the effort? Love, knowing you matter to someone? How many thoughts, as we walk in silence.

Meanwhile, Vadusfadam is even more silent than usual, so much so that he does not reply to our questions.

Then he points something out to us: a cart big enough to transport all of us. It is unattended, attached to two strange beasts similar to horses but with almost human faces. A white one and a brown one.

He has us get in, and while the sun is slowly rising, the cart carries us on our way, jerking us up and down on the road. We were almost better off going on foot ... Perhaps this is another trick of our mysterious Master? Or enchanter?

An Initiate asks, "Is it right to use a means of transport along this path?"

Vadusfadam replies, "It is, provided that we use the time gained to do things we could not do if we were on foot. There is an equilibrium in everything and the pivot of justice is in every aspect. It is up to us not to abuse it. Ours is the power to make laws to be respected, to recognize order from disorder."

Eventually, the road becomes so narrow that the cart cannot go any farther.

There is a sword in the cart, and Vadusfadam hands it to one of us. Then he advises us to pay attention to everything and not to fall asleep, because he will not wake us up, he will leave us behind,. He also tells us to pay careful attention to our steps, where we put our feet, because along this stretch of road – being volcanic in nature and hence also subject to earthquakes – it is easy to twist an ankle in the nasty cracks.

The Monk then sets free the two strange animals, and he has the wheels removed from the cart. He says this is because it has reached the end of its journey. And he rolls the two wheels down the narrow slope: One lands in a gaping crevice almost straight away, while the other carries on, springing right round the bend, down to the bottom without falling over.

We go on, perhaps for hours, until we come across the wheel again. It is stuck, perfectly upright, in a crevice that is almost as deep as its diameter. We are very thirsty, and we notice that above the wheel, spring water gushes forth. The force of the impact has freed the water.

Thus, Vadusfadam tells us, "Strength can express itself in usefulness. But force expressed for power and for selfish ends brings ruin. If you are looking for personal power on this road, you have made a mistake. Turn back while you still have time.

"Right now, for a minute, you have one last chance to change your mind. Those who carry on will have to sacrifice themselves. They will have to forget about themselves; they will not be able to do things only for the ones they love, but for everyone, without distinction. Otherwise, they will lose even that which they believe they have found up to now.

"Whoever does not seek, is inevitably found by death. Not the death which renews – that which turns substances into higher forces and physical flesh into simpler forms – but simply the reaper, which does not distinguish young shoots of grass from old grass.

"You will be overtaken with misfortune, with fear, with selfishness, if you do not make progress and do not make the appointment each of you has in time."

It is the first time Vadusfadam tells us we have an "appointment" somewhere. If that is the case, then I can understand all this hurry to keep going. Or rather, I sense it.

Now we are all more in control, cooler. We try to adapt to the situation. One of my companions says, "Since we've come this far, we may as well go for it."

"But really go for it," the Monk adds. He also invites us to be more relaxed, not to be always worrying about tomorrow. "Take it easy," he says, "and live for now. Know how to mingle without presumption. Water can be too hot or too cold, especially on this volcano. Only mixed can it be used to rinse your eyes."

What an example ... for me cold water is perfectly fine.

Now the sun has reached midday. High above, it shines down on our heads. It is hot, but the Monk does not hint at any kind of break.

Some are tired, and the more tired they are, the more they are resentful toward Vadusfadam. Haste is fine, but a little break every now and then would allow us to rest and then continue with more speed than before. Murmuring among ourselves, some incite resentment in the ranks.

But the Time Monk urges us on, at times even with physical force. I felt really bad when I saw him push one fellow. But is he not a Master, a kind of Saint? If so, shouldn't he conduct himself without vices or weaknesses, and above all without these outbursts of anger, so unexpected and apparently unjustified?

But what is a Master? One who understands something more? An envoy sent from who knows where, to lead us into some promised land?

Promised?

Now that I think about it, Vadusfadam has not promised us anything! What if he isn't a wise man, a great envoy of good? What if he is exactly the opposite?

But if that were the case, wouldn't he try to trick us by always showing his best side, until we were too far down the road to escape ...

But then again, his indifference toward our dead companions and his harshness at certain moments indicate that he could be the Lord of Passions – the very instigator of discord and of all those things he seems to be teaching us to avoid!

This and other conversations we have along the way ...

We move on.

Now the landscape is even wilder than before, one narrow footpath after another above dark precipices. Stone bridges, a hellish landscape.

A little group of those who are most annoyed has stayed slightly behind so as to talk without the Monk hearing. They are a few steps behind me as I finish crossing a bridge.

One of them slips on a loose stone. And now something else is happening: The stone bridge begins to collapse!

The Initiates who are still on the bridge are bewildered. Then one of them lunges toward us and clings onto the rock with his fingers so as not to slide down into the abyss. He screams, while the others disappear below, bouncing off the rocks.

The tragedy, so swift, is frightening. We are all very shocked. I am holding out my hands to help my fallen companion, when Vadusfadam reaches us. He stops me from completing the rescue. While my companion's fingers begin to lose their grip, the Monk squats on his heels and questions him.

With wide eyes we watch the scene. We would like to intervene, but something holds us back. At long last, Vadusfadam stretches out his hand and pulls our friend to safety.

While we are still feeling inside us the echo of the tragedy that has only just happened, Vadusfadam decides to talk to us of ideals, of hope. "Do you remember the shooting star, last night? What did it mean to each one of you? Are you capable of idealizing, of dreaming and so yearning for what is beyond? If you lose strength, aim toward this objective.

"On this journey, do not lose yourself in details when they are not essential. Often they are a trick of your own mind. You think of little things to argue about and you forget what really counts. Instead, try to bring out the creative ability of everyone, the winning energy of the collective imagination."

The moon has set at last. Tomorrow it will rise late, or rather, tonight ... if the night comes.

Maybe it is because I'm tired, but I am seeing strange things: the shadow of those who fell, two dogs in the distance, a large river shrimp in a creek. I blink my eyelids, and everything disappears. It is my mind that has amended reality, hiding those things I seemed to see, and yet ...

We have been awake for a very long time. Despite the fact that we have not slept at all during the long night just passed, at the most dozed, I feel better. Even my tiredness has passed. They say that when you can't make it anymore, when you really can't, that's exactly when unexpected energy bursts forth and manifests within you.

The light that falls on us seems to nourish us, like trees full of leaves. It allows me to arrange events in a clearer light, without always thinking about my position in relation to them. I feel inspired and unexpected intuitions come to me. I literally feel reborn.

I see that the others, too, are feeling something similar. Perhaps they are sounding the call of our redemption.

We continue on.

Now the road is crossing plains. We are in a great expanse of green, barren in parts. The path has become wider, paved with large, flat stones. As yet, we have not come across other travelers.

Vadusfadam is more talkative now, as the evening closes in. It will be a very beautiful sunset. At last, he allows us to set up camp in a wide clearing that is sheltered from the evening wind.

A rather strange thing: There are provisions in this place. There is already some wood for the fire and blankets. At long last, those of us who are left sit down.

Meanwhile the sky is ablaze with red. I cannot remember a sunset like this. All the colors, all the splendor of the sky in the west. Clouds chasing one another, the sun crowned with pink, indigo, and violet.

We are here, sitting down as in a theater. When the sunset is over, we applaud.

Now that it is evening and the fire lit, we get ready to eat. And perhaps we will sleep, but with one eye open.

The night is warm, the fire crackling. I sigh, I feel good. I breathe deeply: one, two, three, four times.

Vadusfadam tells us to sleep, now that we have eaten. We will take turns as guards, a couple of us, every two hours. He will wake up those who are to do the first shift. I am tired, but I'm not sleepy like I expected.

What kind of adventure is this? We set off following the Time Monk, and in so doing we have found ourselves following a non-existent road, marked out in space before the creation of the mountain over which it will cross.

Since leaving this morning our lives have changed. It has been a very long day, and tragic events have transpired. How many of us will survive this adventure?

Someone is already sleeping. Others are late in nodding off. It almost seems that sleeping is a duty, a habit to obey at all costs.

Vadusfadam, standing over us, says that we will follow him also in our sleep, along roads we cannot tread with our feet.

I fall asleep at last ...

FIRST DREAMS

I dream of a great expanse of wheat. Red poppies wave among the ears, while a ruddy cheeked peasant, with a frank, sincere face, advances between the rows of a nearby vineyard. He has a sharpened scythe in his hand.

I feel he is an honest man, well intentioned. But upon reaching some of my companions, he lifts the scythe as if to strike us.

Those who raise their arms to defend themselves have their hands cut clean off. Those who do not move are unhurt.

Behind our backs, a monstrous serpent which was about to strike us has been beheaded. The peasant has saved us. Or rather, he has saved those who trusted him, and has involuntarily wounded those who did not.

I wake up.

Others have had the same dream as I. We recount it, even though it is still the middle of the night.

We are no longer sleepy, and so in groups of three we exchange our stories of the images we dreamed.

The second group dreamed about a lovely woman sitting in a huge field that had just been sown. The woman has some seeds in her hand, which she is counting carefully. Finally, she kneels on the ground and sows them, one by one, after putting them to her forehead for a moment. She says they are her children.

The third group has dreamt that we will leave soon, because we are being followed by a mysterious black creature.

Vadusfadam listens carefully to the telling of our dreams, and on being informed of this last one, gathers all of us together in a mad hurry. He seems agitated, I would even say frightened. Him, frightened?

This thought creates even more commotion among us. In silence we collect our things and we set off on the dark footpath.

Meanwhile the moon comes out quite unexpectedly. Red, huge, then smaller and white. Thanks to its ghostly light we have a chance of not tripping up.

Vadusfadam is a little further ahead of us. At times he turns back and urges us to walk faster. He is brusque, on edge, almost rude with those who slow down. He looks carefully at us one by one, staring us straight in the eye. They say he can read eyes like newspaper pages.

During this night time move things seem stranger than usual. The unknown looms before all of us. Vadusfadam walks on, leaning on a long, crook-handled walking stick.

Every sound is amplified in the night. We have the sensation of being followed. It is an impression that gets stronger minute by minute.

We *are* being followed. Something is behind us, in the night.

A grey mist has descended upon everything. It dims the moon making it reddish, but of a dirty, sickly red. An icy wind drives us on, carrying unknown smells. I don't know if it is the cold or fear, but my back feels like it is naked, unprotected.

We are almost running.

In the distance, as I turn around, I can make out dark shapes, indistinct but certainly not friendly. The Monk has us gather in silence behind a large boulder, so as to hide.

Time goes by.

We hear cries, panting, low, hollow noises, cold as ice. Not far from us dark figures come into view. I recognize among them one of our dead companions who turned back. He is alive! On impulse I almost show myself, because right now I am happy to see him again.

Vadusfadam tries to stop me, but it is too late. My former companion has noticed the movement and has seen me. He shouts something to someone, pointing at me. The wild cries are getting louder, and a dark massive shape rushes in our direction.

The Monk has us hold hands, all of us. He says we must be strong. We must fill our minds with pleasant thoughts, with happiness. We must remember beautiful things.

A bright, colored flood of thought flows out from us. Fluctuating, it offers some resistance to the unleashed rush of the dark shadows.

And so they slow down. They move as if in a swimming pool, but more slowly. It seems they do not like our pleasant thoughts.

In this way we become even stronger, so much so that the black figures start moving as if they were made of rubber, and it is difficult for them to advance.

Now a mental picture has been created, an illusion: images of ourselves that seem to be leaving the shelter, running at a breakneck speed over to the left. The dark shapes leap to chase the illusion, mistaking it for us.

The Time Monk says our holographic images will last for some time, at least long enough to allow us to go a little farther.

We are soaked in sweat. It is difficult to hold our concentration for so long, to move from one lovely thought, already well worn out, to another. We search our memories for other pleasant occasions.

For the moment, we have diverted the Dark Force, which we now instinctively identify as the Enemy.

Presently, we set off again at a swift gait. Around us we can dimly make out the most amazing countryside:

vineyards, meadows, far away cottages immersed in the moonlit night. What a feeling of peace! So different from the events that happened earlier! As though a birth took place just a day ago, and all the anxiety of waiting has disappeared.

Now eight of us are left. We step out, leaning on walking sticks, as though copying Vadusfadam will give us more strength, greater security along this road.

But how long is this path?

Days, nights that never end. Dangers, unexpected changes we have to adapt to, lest they overwhelm us.

Meanwhile, we can hear a distant sound, always the same, not yet identifiable. Just over there, in the night, in front of us.

After the danger we have escaped, we feel like we are reborn, innocent, our hearts and minds open to higher goals. It is a profound, intimate feeling, etched deep inside each one of us. It is so strong that we break the silence and begin to talk to each other while walking through the night.

The moon is high now, and the sky is beginning to turn pale. The noise in front of us is becoming more intense. It seems to be fast flowing water.

As dawn breaks, we still feel reborn, even though we know that our Enemy has certainly taken up our pursuit again.

As we march, we aim at organizing ourselves. And we come to an agreement among us as to what to do in the event of an attack.

Finally we reach the banks of a very wide, swirling river. We have to cross it, Vadusfadam tells us. But how?

By building a raft? There are not enough trees around. By wading across? The water is too swift, full of whirlpools.

Vadusfadam makes us gather some of the thick grass and weave it into mats. I don't know what he wants to achieve, since I don't believe the mats, for their part, are capable of floating, let alone supporting us.

Time goes by ... already the sun has been up for a while. We are afraid our pursuers might arrive, but meanwhile we carry on weaving the grass as asked to do.

Is this a useless task? What has it to do with crossing the water?

Suddenly a shout. Someone has seen something up river: a sort of large raft steered by six individuals with long poles. They are merchants and they are coming down the river they call "Of Time" in search of trade.

They see our mats, woven from grass and flowers, and they offer us passage in exchange for them. Vadusfadam agrees. I have the impression he was waiting for them.

We climb on the bobbing raft, while from afar the screams of our dark pursuers are closing in. Then, just as we push off from the bank, the Enemy appears at the bend!

Now, Dear Reader: Pay Special Attention

Tell me: What time is it now? Because as of now the minutes matter. Write the time down in this space _____ (e.g.: 11:52), and then read thus:

"There are now _____ and _____ pieces of gold (e.g., 11 and 52 pieces of gold) placed in the middle of the raft, more than I would need to be rich. Each one of them represents something:

The first piece of gold is	**PRAISE**
Two pieces of gold are	**PRECISION**
Three pieces of gold are	**INDIVIDUALITY**
Four pieces of gold are	**STRENGTH**
Five pieces of gold are	**INDEPENDENCE**
Six pieces of gold are	**CREDIT**
Seven pieces of gold are	**WAITING**
Eight pieces of gold are	**MATURITY**
Nine pieces of gold are	**CONDESCENDENCE**
Ten pieces of gold are	**LIGHTNESS**
Eleven pieces of gold are	**ATTENTION**
Twelve pieces of gold are	**FAR SIGHTEDNESS**
Thirteen pieces of gold are	**WILL**
Fourteen pieces of gold are	**INDIFFERENCE**
Fifteen pieces of gold are	**MODESTY**
Sixteen pieces of gold are	**IRONY**
Seventeen pieces of gold are	**CUNNING**
Eighteen pieces of gold are	**TALKATIVENESS**
Nineteen pieces of gold are	**BRILLIANCE**
Twenty pieces of gold are	**LOVE**
Twenty-one pieces of gold are	**DISSATISFACTION**
Twenty-two pieces of gold are	**JEALOUSY**
Twenty-three pieces of gold are	**ARROGANCE**
Twenty-four pieces of gold are	**SPIRITUALITY**
Twenty-five pieces of gold are	**LUCK**
Twenty-six pieces of gold are	**WEALTH**
Twenty-seven pieces of gold are	**INTENTION**
Twenty-eight pieces of gold are	**CALCULATION**
Twenty-nine pieces of gold are	**RIGOR**
Thirty pieces of gold are	**SAVING**
Thirty-one pieces of gold are	**AVARICE**
Thirty-two pieces of gold are	**LAZINESS**
Thirty-three pieces of gold are	**GENEROSITY**

Thirty-four pieces of gold are	**INVESTMENT**
Thirty-five pieces of gold are	**MEMORY**
Thirty-six pieces of gold are	**PATHWAY**
Thirty-seven pieces of gold are	**PLEDGE**
Thirty-eight pieces of gold are	**TORTUOUS ROAD**
Thirty-nine pieces of gold are	**PYRAMID**
Forty pieces of gold are	**APPLICATION**
Forty-one pieces of gold are	**OPEN MIND**
Forty-two pieces of gold are	**CLOSED MIND**
Forty-three pieces of gold are	**INTUITION**
Forty-four pieces of gold are	**SYNCHRONICITY**
Forty-five pieces of gold are	**OPPORTUNITIES**
Forty-six pieces of gold are	**ENERGY**
Forty-seven pieces of gold are	**INVENTIVENESS**
Forty-eight pieces of gold are	**DEFENSE**
Forty-nine pieces of gold are	**CONSTRUCTING**
Fifty pieces of gold are	**HERITAGE**
Fifty-one pieces of gold are	**STUDY**
Fifty-two pieces of gold are	**READ EVERYTHING UP TO HERE AGAIN**
Fifty-three pieces of gold are	**CHOSEN COLOR**
Fifty-four pieces of gold are	**HARDNESS**
Fifty-five pieces of gold are	**THE HANDS**
Fifty-six pieces of gold are	**THE EYES**
Fifty-seven pieces of gold are	**THE HEART**
Fifty-eight pieces of gold are	**THE WAY**
Fifty-nine pieces of gold are	**THE AWAKENED SOUL**
Zero Zero pieces of gold are	**ALL IS**

"It is not material wealth that interests me. It is that which I can take with me forever – even after death – that matters to me now."

Meanwhile the raft, little by little, crosses the river diagonally.

On the other side, we find more cultivated fields, orchards, vineyards. Everything indicates that we are close to some city or a large village.

Our band gets going again, while the ferrymen, in spite of our requests, make ready to go back across the river in order to carry over whoever is waiting on the other bank – the Enemy! They agree only to delay their crossing a bit, but we are not sure that they really will.

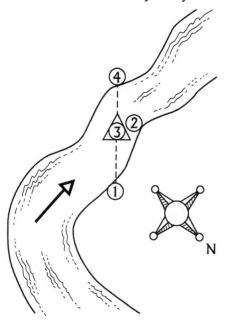

(1) The Enemy, panting
(2) Us, crossing the daytime river
(3) Gold stands out among us,
        interrogating us
(4) The other bank grows closer

By now we are well and truly a travelling community. We hastily try to put as much distance as possible between ourselves and our pursuers.

The sun is high, but not one of us is thinking about stopping to eat. We are all aware of being chased.

Perhaps because danger is so near, we all feel more united, aware and ready to courageously begin this venture to which we feel obscurely called.

We will face every effort with daring. Every endeavor will be made to accomplish ends that are as yet obscure. We will follow Vadusfadam anywhere.

We feel detached now, distant from the things we have left behind: a way of life, all said, that was peaceful, comfortable, almost happy even.

Underneath, some kind of indefinite, unexpressed regret gnaws us. Perhaps even a little sadness. What have we left behind, and for what? Those whom we knew, friends of a thousand games. Things we knew, dreams barely sketched.

And what of us remains outside? A memory that is fading away, an ever longer pause when someone says our name, before it is remembered. They will always remember us in the past: who we were, whose children we were, or whose friends.

Certainly we are not immortal yet. And who is more alone than those who become so?

One fellow is leaning on a walking stick beside the Monk. What do I know of that Initiate? That he appeared among us one day?

And the rest of us, who were we to arrive that same day? How did we cross the Master's path and change ours?

Perhaps it was some dim inner yearning which led us to certain literature. Or a fascination for mysticism. Or insecurity. Or the wish to finally see a better world. Maybe a dream, a memory, recurrent or not, of another incomplete life ...

The fact remains that now we are here.

Here, among ourselves, we have gone from strangers to friends, from friends to brothers and sisters.

Still, some pain exists for things left behind – more for the idea of them than for the things themselves.

It is known that memory changes reality: especially if it was incomplete.

We go on.

It is as if the scenery was created on purpose for us, only for us. A cause that creates an origin, and everything takes shape in front of us.

Where our gaze falls, there are objects that perhaps did not exist prior to our awareness. Like being born, or being continually reborn, we are here to discover the world. Everyone is king with their own cup in their hand.

From our eyes, light. Perhaps a little at a time, our awareness grows. Science that is born from observation.

And within, we begin to know right from wrong at long last. We start to understand how to weigh, in our royal cups, the talents and the true souls of artists, how to distinguish integrity from appearance. More aware, we sense a purpose to all of this, yet it is still unclear.

Nevertheless, we slowly are acquiring the security of having a firm point of reference.

We are still on the road as the sun starts to go down.

Now, the sun has almost set, but Vadusfadam pushes us on more than ever. The sky blazes with red, and we catch a glimpse of a large tree on the horizon. We hurry to reach it.

As we get closer, we notice how tall and broad it is. Night draws in, but we feel safe under the leafy branches of this great tree.

The Monk strokes the tree for a very long time. All of a sudden, a passageway opens at the foot of the tree. Curious and a little apprehensive, we go into the trunk one at a time.

We go down a spiral staircase, which seems to go on forever. We have reached the roots of the tree.

We have made it.

A warm place awaits us, a protected space to sleep. Right in the middle of this great underground hall is a fire without smoke. Huddled together, we look at one another in amazement.

Sitting down, we talk to each other in a rush, more out of relief than out of need for communication. How wonderful it is to be able to do so.

Everyone has a goblet of wine in their hand, and we reflect on our adventure.

Many compare notes they made in the last few days, ponder them, formulate hypotheses, and from them prepare questions to ask Vadusfadam. The Monk answers everyone, and many new topics are discussed.

We wash in the spring that gushes out near a large root; the water is not cold.

What work awaits us? Do we ourselves know what we are looking for? And what will we dream tonight?

Vadusfadam tells us not to fear our Enemies. They cannot enter here, the tree can drive them away.

Furious blows reach our ears from above. To drown them out, we begin playing on hollow roots, like drums. And may our joy, our being together send away and drive off our Enemies.

Joy, set yourself free in our hearts! Rise up, grow, show yourself in our songs, in our dances, in our jokes with one another. In this way, we will be better friends, more trustworthy, closer. And our union will, perhaps, bear lasting fruit.

Already someone is dreaming of a village that is all ours, a place where we can live, study, grow, and become old together. Our homeland is growing!

After all, are we not citizens of the world? With no more identity, we want to create a new civilization that will open up evolutionary roads for Humankind. New experiments, research within each one of us, until we locate the deep hidden fire which animates us.

We dream of victory without having yet fought. We imagine ourselves triumphant, developing a distinct and superior new culture.

There are those who recite, who go off to prepare a little play. Still others try again the dance steps they have only just learned. Some play music instinctively, others sing. Our games become more organized, a bit at a time.

Outside the moon has surely risen. But tonight we have a home! Tomorrow, who knows?

Sleep gathers us up one at a time, like ripe fruit. Vadusfadam has taught us what to do in order to dream and travel in our astral bodies with him. He will take us to fight, when we are ready.

I dream of a very beautiful female face, gentle, bewitching. Her femininity is exalted by the feeling of modesty that she emanates. The woman lifts her hands to her face, and hides. Why? Why does she deprive me of her beauty? What is it that hampers her?

There is a figure behind her, a smiling male figure. Now she is no longer looking at the red fire, which both separated and united us. She has turned toward her companion and the shadow conceals her face.

When I awake, I immediately recount the dream I have had to others. Indeed, I am curious to discover if anyone shared it with me.

And other companions relate their dreams to me. Some tell of finding themselves immersed up to the waist in a shallow lake. Above this mirror of water, colored birds fly very low, each with a name on its breast: *Imagination, Soul, Intelligence.*

The flying creatures chase one another, mingle and draw figures in the air. Every now and then, they dive into the water and come out with a precious stone in their beaks. Then they fly above the people immersed in the water and drop these jewels on them.

Another group had a dream about a drought-ridden, barren place where very old people are forever strolling, each with a small snake coiled on their left shoulder.

Vadusfadam says it is the place of eternal memory, where people who are afraid of getting old and who take refuge in their memories, futilely burn themselves out.

It is the road to the eternal past, where memories, rather than being the sum of experience, bring only regrets. And the regrets are embodied by those serpents, larvae that feed on the ghost of life gone by.

He then talks about how our ideal city should be built, in his opinion. Above all, a place designed to preserve and perpetuate our inner discoveries. A place to spread the light, with firm belief, of the ideas that excite us. A place where we can create traditions and develop, by continual application, the abilities of everyone who is modest and big-hearted enough not to be proud.

Will we be able to give ourselves laws that are intimate and minimalistic, yet sagacious and strong? Will we be able to respect them? Will we evolve enough to implement the lessons and legacy of the Time Monk?

These and other conversations occupy us for now.

The night deepens. The hours go by slowly, and the fire never goes out.

Some are worried, anxious. Others are bored and throw little stones into the fire. It is not fatigue, but a kind of regret, a feeling of incompleteness that pervades us.

Like black fingers, a subtle, misty, creeping darkness filters through from above. Vadusfadam tries to shake us out of it, but the uneasiness remains.

Our minds are strange: They work if given continual injections of activity, but immediately afterward, they lose concentration – the pressure that is indispensable to travel the road toward the Central Fires.

At least that is what Vadusfadam says, but we don't even know what the Central Fires are.

We ask him, and as he talks, little by little we come around. We wake up from this sleepiness, this unhealthy torpor that was sucking our souls dry ...

Part Two
The Second Scarlet Door

In the center of the world, down there where all caravans lead, where the light is created instant upon instant, there is the Land of Fires.

There, the fires are alive. They burn but they do not consume, they dance eternally, they keep the material universe alive.

Seven Scarlet Doors must be passed through to reach them. We stepped beyond the First Door, invisible, when we ventured along the path on the mountain that is not born yet.

The Second Door is on this side of the river, a little beyond the tree which shelters us. At the right time, and only then, will it be possible to pass through it.

The Fires down there, in that infinite valley, meld with each other. To the wanderer they look like the lights of a huge army encampment.

All travelers who reach the Central Fires leave their own small or great fire alive forever in that place. Inextinguishable, it will be a beacon for them, from one life to another.

It is our task to add our fires to the central ones.

The road we are on leads there. In making this journey, we will complete an essential cycle. We will allow the heart of Humankind to take another beat.

Down there, all roads, human and non-human, knot together. There, humanity – this divided, humiliated, broken, lobotomized, downtrodden race – may rise up again fighting.

To win back our souls we must pass through the Seven Scarlet Doors. Fixed passageways, difficult, cruel at times, never without their price.

We are struggling against attentive intelligences, ready to pick up on every mistake of humanity, to take, and to maintain an advantage.

This is not just any game we are playing. Or at least, the Game of Life is not an innocent game. Innocence was broken into pieces forever when our species was tricked and defeated.

Will we recover? Will we rise again?

How many more will try to cross those powerful Doors that separate us from ourselves, but which, at least, define our most intimate boundaries inside chaos.

A few? Many?

Vadusfadam says that the caravans are already coming to an end. Ours is one of the last, in this final age. Beyond a certain point in time, fighting back would be useless.

Meanwhile, as Humankind tries to reawaken, its Enemy hounds and pursues it as long as it is weak and divided, like our group.

And so many fall along the way!

Sure of themselves, seekers of security and gratification, they are often tricked. They do not know how to recognize truth from falsehood. They give in just a few steps away from reaching their goal.

And the Enemy rejoices in its own way, feeding on our pain at every defeat inflicted upon us, in small things as well as the big ones.

Words not honored, lies, craftiness which no one is supposed to notice, are all wounds in our weakest spots.

We need love. So much love, in every possible guise.

Friendship, which is love among men or women. Passion, which is explosive love between a man and woman. And then every other shade in between.

This is a powerful weapon against our Enemy.

When two people link arms and raise their drinking cups together, they trust one another, they stand back-to-back in danger. Then there is love, attraction to each other. And there is also defense, looking out for each other,

It works at all ages. It is the driving force of the highest aim of our souls.

But a dangerous Enemy knows how to take advantage even of this and turn it against us! Whenever love becomes troubled – bound up with egoism, with lack of trust and possessiveness, with morbidity that makes beauty turn pale and changes joy into captivity – then tears take the place of smiles. Torment, suspicion, pain are constantly felt.

To love in pain!

Vadusfadam now asks us to eat again. Already our meals, our sleeping habits, everything, I should say, has become irregular ...

And yet afterward this will seem like an important meal, a ritual meal.

Strangely we all have an appetite. And there is no shortage of food. Who arranged it for us? And who lit the fire before our arrival? Who gathered the wood to stoke it?

So far we have not seen anyone, and yet chores have been done. Who is our mysterious host?

Now the Time Monk asks us to hurry up, since he says there is still a long way to go.

By this time our pursuers must have fallen into that strange sleep, where they feed on nightmares and cannot follow.

However, as we are about to leave, Vadusfadam stops suddenly, turns around and directs a harsh gaze at us. "Is this the way," he asks, "to leave the house that has given us hospitality? Thus do we repay the generosity of the one who arranged everything for us?"

He has some Initiates put down what little baggage they are still carrying, and he orders us to tidy up the great room inside the tree: sweep the floor; put everything in its place; each one of us has to feed a little stick of wood to the living Central Fire. We are mortified we didn't think of it ourselves.

"Even with danger upon us," he adds, "a mess is not to be allowed. It attracts the Enemy, as honey attracts flies."

We tidy up quickly.

Then, one at a time, we leave the safety of the tree and go out into the open. We pass through a well hidden door between two great roots. We are lower down in relation to the entrance, because the ground slopes downward.

Thus we notice that the tree stands in a rather deep gully.

In the darkness, we set off in a line along a path that is feebly lit by the stars.

(1) *Our Enemies are waiting for us*
(2) *Us in the sheltered room*
(3) *The exit into the gully*

In the depths of the night, we catch a glimpse at the bottom of the gully of the famous Second Scarlet Door that Vadusfadam had been telling us about. It looks like a stepped pyramid with a narrow passageway in the middle.

We go nearer: Two seated statues armed with swords face each other. One male, one female.

The pyramid and the statues are painted red. Or perhaps the very stones from which they are made are this color.

As the distance between us, still in single file, lessens, the statues appear more majestic.

On the flat summit of the pyramid burns a fire such as I have never seen. It is scarlet red in color, and little flames of the same color rain down, like a waterfall, in front of the Door.

Vadusfadam urges us to move quickly, until we are in front of this strange portal. He gathers us together in a circle and tells us this is the passageway from which there is no more turning back.

He states, "The female statue represents justice, the careful and measured diligence of our travelled path. The male statue betokens the threat of proceeding with the journey, the deprivations that will befall us, the sacrifices that we will surely have to make if we continue."

At the foot of the female statue flows a stream of lava. At the foot of the male statue, there are shields, broken lances, stained and rusty suits of armor.

Vadusfadam looks straight at us, one by one. He has something difficult to tell us, that is clear.

He has us line up side-by-side, eight good paces from the Door after measuring them out. He draws a horizontal line in front of the group, and then individual lines in front of each one of us that lead to the threshold of the portal.

In response to his eloquent mapping, we get on the ground on our hands-and-knees and face the Scarlet Door.

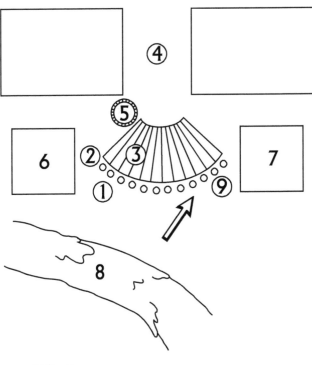

(1) Us
(2) The starting line
(3) Each person's track
(4) The Second Scarlet Door
(5) Vadusfadam
(6) Female statue
(7) Male statue
(8) Stream of lava
(9) Rusty weapons

In a moment, we will have to move slowly toward the Door, as slowly as possible and without stopping. We will need to focus all our awareness on our senses. And it is essential that we perceive with *all* our senses – every object that we come across, great or small, in every shape or form, between here and the Scarlet Door.

And whoever gets there first will be the loser.

Therefore, this is our battle: We must move as slowly as possible. We cannot stop. We must perceive with the utmost intensity every object, every grain or tiny stone, every insect or twig that we come across on our path. And we must not be the first one through the Door ...

But does that mean we want to be last?

I no longer wonder if what we are doing has any value or not. I simply put all of myself into the challenge I am asked to undertake.

And my companions do the same.

This, in spite of knowing that the Enemy is close on our heels.

The Time Monk gives the go-ahead to this bizarre competition.

I set off. I am touching. I am brushing against. I am trying to feel with all of my body. All senses alert!

I am moving forward very, very slowly. Some Initiates are faster; others are going more slowly than I.

I am sweating, as if running breathlessly. It is difficult. At every moment I risk losing my concentration.

The Door is getting nearer now. The little flames cascading down from above seem slower.

Suddenly, a new thought: I tell myself that I am struggling *with* my companions, not against them. In this strange way, I am not actually fighting them. We are fighting *for* each other.

I slow down, I speed up. On all fours, I adjust my pace to the speed of the others. Now, I would like us all to get there together. The door is probably wide enough for our group. However, I do not want to be the first.

Stones, earth, bits of straw. Colors, smells, sweat. Weariness, cramped muscles.

I must even observe the beads of my sweat dripping into the dust.

Under the light of the stars, hours seem to go by. Perhaps day is dawning, since the shadows are lighter.

It means the Enemy will see us and be able to catch up with us.

We now are in front of the doorway – those were the eight longest steps of my life!

I see the low flames raining down from the fire. I feel their heat on my face.

We continue to move forward. I sense that we are lined up in a row.

The fire runs over me, but it does not burn. Yet, if I lose my concentration, even for just a second, the heat immediately becomes unbearable.

"Calm down, stay calm," I tell myself. "Breathe, there, like this."

I feel the air in my nostrils ... the earth under my hands ... the sweat dripping ... the fire that does not scorch ...

We went through!

Together!

Quickly, Vadusfadam makes us move on, walking once again, but no talking.

So I privately reflect: The miracle is that we all reached the door at the same moment! The fastest ones managed to wait; the slowest managed to adjust to the ones in front.

The Time Monk watches us attentively, with curiosity. He himself is amazed at our achievement.

We are proud of ourselves.

But other eyes are watching us beyond the Door – those of thousands upon thousands of animals, of every kind, all turned toward us.

They do not show any fear or animus. Only curiosity. They seem to be appraising us, weighing us. Then they go away in silence. They never came close enough to be touched.

I turn around.

Seen from this side, the Second Scarlet Door is a narrow cleft in the mountainside. And where we saw the fire on the top, now there is a large glacier.

Vadusfadam says that in order to follow us, the Enemy will have to climb the glacier or go around the mountain. Therefore, we will have some respite.

Meanwhile, dawn has fully broken, rose-colored, as always on this journey.

We continue along the road, and I think about what we have left behind in the world from which we came ...

Clouds are gathering further ahead. A cold wind draws them together, as a dog does the flock. Perhaps it will rain.

The trek is steadily uphill, but not noticeably so or that difficult. Perhaps we are "finding our legs," as they say.

I have lost all notion of time. I do not know any more how long it is since we set off. Perhaps I didn't even know before.

Regrets? I don't think so. I may have chosen on impulse, but I decided on my own to go down this road. Better than never deciding, out of fear of facing something new or of losing my possessions.

I must not pine or feel remorse. I am an adult, and I wanted to do what I have done.

Rather than worrying, it is important to carry on. Every choice, every fundamental moment is always, only ever, NOW!

As we walk, Vadusfadam answers our endless questions. Some are very important, others trivial. But how do you decide what is trivial for one person and fundamental for another? We are not all the same.

Indeed, the Monk says that no two of us are alike and that everybody is extremely important for everyone else, that we complement one another.

He then talks about what is essential for each person, about how everyone always sees things solely from his or her own point of view. He calls it the "quasi-real."

We ask him, as the sun rises in the sky, if there are others like him. And what does "Time Monk" mean.

"Yes," he says, "there is an order of Monks to which I belong. And this is the definition you can best understand. We are beings from different worlds, linked together by the soul we share.

"We have many bodies, many contemporaneous appearances in various points of space and time. We travel along Synchronic Lines from one point of life to another.[3]

"We know and deepen our common magic rituals, and it is our aim to join human forces together again. We are guerrillas who, jumping from one time wave to another, one divine present to another, knit together, little by little, the different parts of Cosmic Humanity."

I don't understand all the things he told us, but he assures us that that it will suffice for now and that we will understand a little at a time.

Will we have our own land some day? Will our wandering come to an end, this tiring trek that is taking us to unknown destinations?

Vadusfadam tells us that even if one day we have houses and farms and a great deal of land and items of wealth, luxury, beautiful things we are fond of, we must never be tied to these things. We must always be ready to leave, at any moment. If new stages to our journey develop, it will be up to us to proceed on the path, wherever it may take us.

As long as we have the spirit of movement in us, we will be true seekers. If we stop – because we grow too attached to those we love or to things of value that we have gradually accumulated and built with our physical hands – then the goal will be much farther ahead of us.

---

[3] The Synchronic Lines are rivers of energy that encircle the planet and connect it to the universe. They wind their way horizontally, vertically, deep inside the earth and around the poles, to thought, intuition, dreams, and ways of thinking, enveloping all the planets that host life.

We will be a travelling tabernacle, he says. Like the ancient Hebrew people, we will follow the Ark as it changes places; it will not follow our movements.

True citizens of the world.

Thus, we can never be broken up, because wherever we are, there will be our homeland. The ability to adapt will be our banner, regardless of our age and our role at the time.

We will be careful with our wealth, but also generous, truly willing to give up everything to save what really counts. Thus, not too tied to matter but careful to respect it, we will be able to grow to our full human potential. We will dig deep inside ourselves without fear, since there will be no rubble dangerously piled up at our backs. And we will have the immense wealth of generosity.

In the beginning, we had to struggle with ourselves to bring only the things we felt were absolutely necessary on this journey. Then we realized how heavy they were and how much they slowed us down. We opened our backpacks and chose what were the most important items among what we used to believe was absolutely necessary. And we realized how many useless things we possessed.

Having knotted our bundles again, we set off once more with a lighter load. But even then, after a long anxious trek, we soon discovered how much the weight of our possessions still slowed us down.

We also discovered a strange principle (at least as strange as grace) that regularly comes into play: *Providence.* Or perhaps, it is extraordinary *Synchronicity.*

We found a shelter. And in the shelter, we found food, what we needed to be comfortable, a fire ready lit.

However, it was very difficult for me to accept that this would always happen – to let go of my load, to have total faith, to place my trust in this principle, in providence.

Vadusfadam reminds us that even in the future, if our cause is right, this marvelous, mysterious principle will always apply.

"Just as every creature manages to find food and shelter from the moment it takes that form, the moment it is created, the moment it is born, so we will manage to find everything we feel we need.

"Perhaps someone will save their soul due to their generosity toward us.

"Just as we may save ours by showing generosity toward others. To those who show us generosity with deeds and material goods, we will be generous in return, with far more precious spiritual gifts. Then on other occasions, we will be the hand of providence for others, who, perhaps without knowing, are spiritually generous with us."

He concludes by saying, "This game will go on forever."

Certainly, these things may be true. All true. But other people – those outside our present world – what will they say?

Likely, they will try to convince us we are making a mistake. And they will judge us according to their measure, their space, as limited as an alley, a courtyard. Yes, their territory is narrower than ours, but often their observations may be right.

But we ... are we right? Can there be two opposite views of the world, both correct?

I believed so, before travelling this stretch of road. But now I realize that people's views of reality diverge too much. I realize there are different planes of perception, of values given to objects and to circumstances.

"Chance" no longer exists for me and for the other Initiates.

In every occurrence, we now try to read things that, at first sight, our eyes cannot see. We even try to be critical, with ourselves and with each other. But woe to anyone who takes us all on together!

Can this attitude be right? Maybe it is an essential stage in forming a collective consciousness?

What animates us more than anything else, I believe, is HOPE. That youthful vigor, the desire, as the years go by, to remain clear-eyed. Full of longing for doing, being, without fear of appearing the way others see us, when they mirror themselves in us.

The Master views such people as profiteers, exploiters, crafty and sly.

There is a well known parable about a speck in someone else's eye and a beam in one's own ...

Long live hope!

Better to be naive, to strive to be so, than to steal anything at all, ideas, words, things.

Let us look forward to so much naiveté, my brothers and sisters. A naiveté that lasts, that cannot be seen by others with physical eyes.

The sun is high above our heads.

We stop in a well tended garden. At its entrance is written in stone: "Wanderers' Garden."

Vadusfadam allows us to pick freely of the fruit from the trees, bowed down with the weight of their sweet smelling produce.

Apples, pears, many types of grapes. Walnuts, hazelnuts, figs of all sorts. But he stops us from taking with us more than a single piece of fruit and some water in a few bottles.

We set off on the road again. The road is long and straight now, across a wide plain. It never changes, and no matter how far down the road we go, we always seem to be in the same place.

Some have their feet covered in blisters, but our march cannot slow down. They know it, and they grit their teeth to carry on.

What for us are long hours go by. Very slowly, the sun slides toward the west.

Our march slows down a little, we are tired. Now, someone is complaining about the effort, and the more they talk about it, the more they transfer their state of mind to the others.

Now there is someone crying – someone who wants to stop and shouts, "To hell with it all!" Not even the fear of those chasing us manages to spur us on.

Vadusfadam is silent.

He walks quickly and without slowing down, methodically. We try to keep up with him, but after a while our group has become a broken trail of people dragging themselves along on their own.

One Initiate tries to encourage the others, but her words fall more and more on deaf ears. Another asks how much farther it is until the next stopping place?

The Time Monk replies, "A long way..."

PART THREE
The Third Scarlet Door

We feel shattered. As if all the effort of the past days has caught up with us all of a sudden. We have encountered many tests thus far, but not the tedium of this!

The sun seems to stand still, just hinting at setting. The road is straight and endless. Is this what makes it so difficult to carry on?

As long as there was one difficulty after another, we were continually stimulated by the problems themselves, and by their solutions. Yet now that everything seems easier, even the flat road seems impossible to travel.

We are seriously at risk of failing our mission, whatever it is ...

Vadusfadam does not slow down. He is always there, ahead of us, little by little, further and further away.

Each of us has our own pace, and on a road, so straight and always the same, in a short time people get farther apart from one another.

Then, gradually, the landscape changes. Now there are hillocks, alternating with ditches, as if whoever built the road wanted to avoid cutting into them to flatten the short slopes and inclines.

In a short while I find myself alone. I cannot see anyone either in front of or behind me. And the sun has gone down by an infinitesimal fraction of a degree. Every now and then it is veiled by thick clouds, which have been looming since the morning. Every now and then the shadows get longer and colder.

I go on, accompanied only by the sound of my footsteps, by the hurried beating of my heart, and by the panting of my breath. I am alone. I feel profoundly alone.

Vadusfadam is over there, ahead. He has never slowed down to wait for us. Why?

Meanwhile the sky is darker. The clouds seem to have come to an agreement, and they gather threateningly.

Large drops of rain start to fall, tepid at first. But then the downpour becomes heavy, shuttering down.

I am cold and I can scarcely see anymore, but I continue to move along the road. I can guess only approximately where I am, somewhere on the right-hand side of the road.

I grit my teeth and move on.

One step, another. One more, yet one more. Then I swear to myself that I will stop! But I move on ... again. If only there were someone beside me, perhaps we could encourage one another.

I sharpen my ears, hoping to hear someone coming. I look ahead, but I can't see beyond a few yards.

I am not used to walking for so long. I can't feel my legs any more. The whole of my back aches, and I've got a stitch in my side.

Great, a really fine picture: *The Initiate, he who seeks, brought down by aching feet!*

I go on, though I am wet through and through, soaked to the skin. I fall down and realize I'd prefer to stay on the ground in the puddles and rest.

I cry with rage! I scream till my voice goes! I thump my fists on the ground, with what little strength remains!

But then, with an enormous effort, I get up again.

For me, subjectively speaking, it has been raining for hours. The sky is still dark, but perhaps the rain is coming down a little less than before.

"How long before we stop?" I barely whisper. I no longer have a voice to shout and I doubt anyone can hear me behind these accursed hillocks.

Nobody replies, and I do not have the courage to slow down to wait for some travelling companion. I feel alone, isolated, as if closed in a tomb where no one can help. I feel distant from everything and from everyone.

It has almost stopped raining. A fine, persistent drizzle, November like, is falling from the sky now.

My feet are covered in blisters. I don't take off my shoes because I certainly would not manage to put them on again.

The sun is almost on the horizon from what I can guess, looking for its light behind the clouds.

I move forward. The effort to lift my feet is enormous. I feel heavy, on top of feeling tired. Only will sustains me. I am going down an endless road and I do not know where it leads.

The Time Monk is marching on ahead somewhere, and I can only hope that he has not turned off at a fork I didn't see! This idea frightens me.

I go on, wrapped up in my uncertainty.

What is still keeping me going? Pure will, anger, the obstinacy that says if the others can make it, I too must make it? This is nothing great as far as elevated thoughts go, but be that as it may, I feel a little stronger.

My back may be shattered, but an idea is awakening in me from the words spoken by the Master, which I think about over and over again and which keep me going:

I am someone fortunate.

Yes, a fortunate traveler who is walking, though weak, toward the Central Fires along this dark, challenging road. And I have passed through two of the Scarlet Doors!

These thoughts are heartening and I lift my head up, able to go on a little bit more ...

I walk and I think; I think and I walk.

The sky is clear now. What seems to be a pinnacle appears before me in the distance. A reference point at last!

I keep going with the last of my strength on the road, which still is flat.

I turn around, and nearby there is someone who is trudging on like me. Also ahead, some little moving dots are perhaps my companions.

My heart swells with joy. I feel linked to these people. More than ever I feel they are a part of me.

The pinnacle, a little bigger, is still very far away. The sun has set behind me.

I move on as fast as I can, because I notice that the road branches out in a radius of different directions. If I do not reach that spire in time, I risk losing sight of my companions and the Master, up ahead.

Come on wretched legs, carry me for a little longer! How is it possible that Vadusfadam never slows down?

At times I realize that I have lost my rhythm, that I am slower. I pull myself together, and quicken my pace, just when I think I've reached and exceeded my maximum limit.

I shout, but by now no sound comes out of my parched throat. And I have no more water to quench my thirst.

I dredge up what strength I have left, as if I were scraping the bottom of the barrel. I fall down. I get up and I fall down again.

I begin to crawl along the road. I grab hold of every chink, any bump sticking up as if I were climbing a wall.

I close my eyes. I open them again. Perhaps I have passed out. I try to get up and fail. I find a large stick, and I practically haul myself onto it in order to get myself on my feet.

I move onward, once again, dragging the stick along because I no longer have the strength to carry it in front of me. I drop it. I waver. I have to drag myself along but I manage to go on ...

Then I bump into something.

My eyes are closed, as it has been dark for some time. A hand stops me, makes me sit down, assisting me with care. It is the Time Monk, and he is smiling.

The pinnacle is a very high pole supporting a rope bridge, the end of which I cannot see. As one by one we arrive, disheveled, Vadusfadam tells us we must cross it, alone.

The hanging bridge is made of red ropes. The Monk warns us, as we walk across it, that we will encounter true and false wealth. We must know how to tell the difference.

This is the Third Scarlet Door.

Exhausted, we reach the Monk who gives us this warning: We will find a plain wooden door in the middle of the bridge. We must pass through it before our pursuers get here.

One-by-one, we venture forth onto the bridge. As soon as I put my foot down I can feel it rock; I do not like this at all. I hold on tight to the two ropes that act as hand rails, and, as carefully as I possibly can, I place my feet on the decking, which is made of unsafe little planks with worrying gaps.

I cannot see the bottom of the chasm. I keep going. A cold night wind makes every joint, every part of the bridge creaks. Tired, trembling with the effort, I move onward.

All of this adventure is a crazy race.

In the dark night, only the stars give a little faint light. The moon will rise later.

I walk ... I walk on ... I trip up and get scared. My heart leaps in my mouth, but I carry on.

Then, I see the outline of a figure in front of me. A man, I would say. A short, sturdy man, dressed in a red and black cape now blocks my path.

He demands money to let me pass. I do not have any, and besides, why should I pay him? Is he by chance the owner of the bridge or its keeper?

He says he is, but I feel it is not true. He is a mere trickster who wants to rip someone off. And that someone is me.

I am about to react with harsh words, but I remember Vadusfadam's advice regarding appearing naive, if it seems the right thing to do:

"You can give to him who asks – a person who thinks he is cunning and is trying to trick you – whatever he wants, but it will always be less than he would have honestly earned if only he had the dignity to search for himself."

Is it right to be naive in this instance?

"Okay," I respond. "What can I give you? My belt, my shoes that have lost their shape? What else have I got?"

He points to the ring on my finger.

"This? Isn't it a bit much?" I ask. Then I ponder his demand: I am fond of the ring ... but now, what need do I have of it? I have left everything else behind. Certainly, I would not risk losing myself over a ring, however dear.

I form my answer: "Here, take this old silver chain as well, and the leather belt from my trousers. A piece of string will suffice – I'll be lighter."

I deposit all my loose possessions in his hands, and I see an astonished look on his face when I pass him by. Then he shouts at me to stay to the left on the bridge, because the handrail is worn on the right and broken further ahead.

I move forward, cautiously but quickly.

The bridge is very long and seems to go on forever. I keep to the left.

Much later on, I come across a very beautiful woman, covered in jewejs and very richly dressed. She is seated, balancing on the red rope handrail. She smiles and looks at me.

I draw nearer and she addresses me. She asks who I am and what I am doing there. I tell her I am someone who seeks, someone who does not even know his own name anymore.

She tells me that I have passed enough tests and that if I want, I now can be rich and happy. I can make love to her, sleep in a golden bed, have for myself all the considerable wealth at her disposal, including gold and money, and have everything that I could possibly want in this life. She urges me – in a charming manner and without pressing me too much – to consider her offer.

When I hesitate, she adds that I will have security. Instead of being a vagabond searching for a symbolic, undefined goal, I will have wealth and power, glory for the rest of my life.

Not that I wouldn't like these gifts ... but I quickly realize that I have walked too far down the road to the Central Fires to stop now. Even though her offer tempts me slightly, I shrug my shoulders and pass her by.

At that exact moment, the rope she is sitting on breaks! The woman is hurled into empty space along with her weighty wealth.

I feel too sick, too tired to have pity on her. I wait till the bridge stops rocking, and I move on.

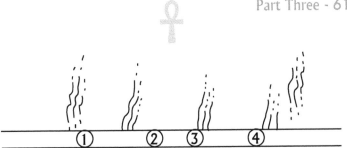

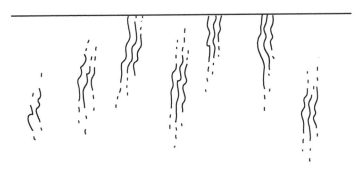

(1) *The bridge*
(2) *He who asks for too much*
(3) *She who offers too much*
(4) *The Third Scarlet Door*

Eventually, I see the Third Scarlet Door. It is a small wooden structure and I am unsure how to open it. There is no handle, nor do I see any hinges on which it can swing.

I push it and shake it, but it does not move. However, if I lean my hands on the door, and if I do it gently, I get the impression that a door batten is being pulled. Thus, by barely touching the door, little by little it lifts up on two invisible sliding tracks.

I also learn that if I put my hands in the free space underneath and pull upward, it does not move. Only if I place the palms of my hands on its surface and I move them up very slowly, does the door lift up, as if pulled by static electricity.

It takes time, but the door opens. I cross the threshold and, immediately, it shuts again.

On the other side of the door, I continue walking. The bridge seems to go on forever. My eyes are closing with fatigue ...

Finally, I reach the end of the bridge and step onto land once more. I am safely past the Third Scarlet Door!

The moon is high; it is waxing. In a few days it will be full.

A little further on, I see a walnut tree and, it seems, a lively fire. A few of my companions have already arrived before me.

I throw myself down on the ground. Every part of me is aching. Someone lifts my head and makes me drink something. It seems like vegetable soup.

I keep my eyes closed and I feel really good. I am fine but I have no desire to move. I fear that if I were to change positions all my muscles would start aching again.

Then I fall asleep.

I can hear voices, people laughing and talking things over. I recognize those sounds, and I manage to visualize the faces of those who are talking.

I get up and I look at them all, one by one. They are recounting their respective experiences. Others, too, met the stocky man and a second figure, similar to the woman I encountered.

I count my travelling companions. A few are missing. I ask if by chance some are already further on ... but the reply is an embarrassed silence.

Vadusfadam says they lost their way, or gave the wrong replies, or are now buried by wealth. He tells us that we have passed an important stage of the journey and gained a certain advantage over our pursuers, which is not to be wasted.

Dawn is breaking.

We eat and then it is time to take to the road again. Fortunately, we are all feeling stronger, and we walk as a group, as brothers and sisters.

While we march, Vadusfadam starts the day's lesson: stresses how important learning is for us. He discusses thousands of topics with us, opening up new pathways in our minds.

He talks to us of chance, of fortune, of the rebirth that each one of us has yet to undergo. And he warns us about what we will find along the next stretch of the road.

"At the Fourth Scarlet Door, you will remember your past lives, and certain aspects of those memories – about yourself, your conduct – will not be pleasant." Beyond that clue, we will be on our own.

"But how long is this stretch of road?" we ask. "When will we get to the next Door?"

"When you are ready, and if you make it there in time," he tells us.

Part Four
The Fourth Scarlet Door

Day has come. The landscape has gradually opened up and has become drier.

We come across a well near an uninhabited house.

We drink, we eat what we find, we clean up everything properly without having to be told, and we set off down the road again. We bring with us several containers of water covered with cloths.

We are tanned and our muscles are stronger. All of us are looking better, and we are not afraid of the desert that is drawing near, perhaps because we are together.

Coming through challenging experiences brings people together more than anything else. Wanting to get involved in a venture – make real something beautiful, something tangible – is the secret goal of everyone.

To succeed, to bring to completion, to make happen! To accomplish what no one yet has tried and gain results that no one else has achieved!

The spirit of achievement and the idea of being part of a group where everyone can trust one another gives us a feeling of omnipotence and wholeness. It widens our horizons.

We talk, we get to know each other, we fantasize together. We are all closer. In an atmosphere of such comradery, the time passes quickly.

It is an unbelievably starry sky that welcomes us tonight. And then the moon rises, a little fuller than last evening.

The vast night is above us, magnificent, glorious. We walk in silence, as if to avoid disturbing the stars.

Unspeakable splendor!

The silver dust of the Milky Way – the wide arm of the spiral of which our little Earth is a part – glistens before our widening eyes. A magical night.

More magical than the very journey we are undertaking? And up there, or over there, do other eyes gaze in our direction?

The Monk whispers that, beyond, there are intelligences that understand us, just as there are those that fear us.

Fear us? Here?

Aren't we far away and small and vulnerable? This tiny blue world – out on the edge, submerged in the living wave of forms, evolutions of species triggered by unimaginable events – could it possibly have such great importance?

Oh, I breathe in this sky, these stars, those distant suns. A meteor slowly showers us with a luminous trail of white dust. It seems to show us the way, over there, down this road, to those mysterious, fascinating Central Fires ...

The Monk invites us to perceive the now, to learn to know the present. Not just the memory of yesterday, but the expectation of tomorrow.

You too, Dear Reader: Pay Attention Once More

Look at what time it is. You can ignore the minutes this time. Which of the twelve hours is it right now? Write the hour here _____.

If it is one o'clock:
Soon, something will make you happy ... if you know where to look.

If it is two o'clock:
Tomorrow, you can expect a sign.

If it is three o'clock:
The animals will bring you advice.

If it is four o'clock:
Your body will talk to your mind

If it is five o'clock:
A dream will lead you onto the path.

If it is six o'clock:
A child is your mirror. Observe it.

If it is seven o'clock:
The words of someone, overheard by chance, will answer you.

If it is eight o'clock:
A building, a monument will bring back memories.

If it is nine o'clock:
Remember to breathe! And then try to laugh.

If it is ten o'clock:
Remember who loves you. There is somebody.

If it is eleven o'clock:
Talk to an elderly person. You will understand, even if they do not.

If it is twelve o'clock:
You will make an agreement with yourself or with others. And you will keep the promise.

We proceed on the road. We feel small, facing this immensity. We move as friends, close to one another.

We walk until the road, all of a sudden, disappears under the sand. Vadusfadam tells us it is up to us to find it again, but that he will continue to follow us as long as we stay together.

We move off, a little hesitant, trying to get our bearings by the stars. Walking in the sand is much more difficult. Treading is slower, tiring. Time goes by ...

Even keeping straight is difficult. Someone thinks we have wandered a little to the right. Others are of the opposite opinion.

Fact is, we are beginning to argue. There is someone who wants to wander off in one direction, is sure of it, while someone else wants to move in the other direction, being just as sure.

We do not know what to do. Then we decide to subjectively establish for our own purposes of navigation what is "right" and "wrong."

Is this our generosity toward each other? The gift we are preparing to offer others? What is the good of possibly parting ways?

Only one thing is clear: Splitting up will do more damage than taking the wrong road.

Each of us has our own conclusions, intuitions, ideas, imagined solutions. Then we vote by a show of hands, choosing who may try to guide us.

It falls to a woman.

However reluctant and full of doubt, having chosen this method, we let her guide us ...

More time goes by and day is dawning. We can't have gone far wrong, if we are heading toward the sunrise.

Vadusfadam, who is following us in silence, moves forward now and leads us in a determinate direction, slightly over to the right. Then he hangs back again to the rear of our caravan.

As by agreement, come sunrise, we again choose by a show of hands who will guide us until midday, provided we do not find the road before then.

It falls to the same woman again!

So we follow her. Every now and then, the Monk gives us some brief advice.

The sun has now risen and it beats hard, with fury, upon our heads. Our breaks become more frequent, and Vadusfadam no longer prods us on.

Time passes slowly, the heat grows. And yet we feel it is very important to stop and discuss, more calmly now, what direction to take.

We eat something, sharing it in brotherly fashion. A few apples, some other pieces of fruit. I am hungry and share my provisions.

When the sun begins to lower and a light but persistent wind comes up, we do not slow down, even though our eyes are stinging from the sand. Sand is everywhere! In the nose, in the throat, all over us. One dune after another, we slip and slide whether going up or down, laboring a great deal. But we move on.

The goal has more importance than any one of us. Thus we do not spare ourselves.

The wind is getting stronger and we are forced to halt. We no longer have any point of reference.

Meanwhile, it turns to evening, and by night the wind stops. Here are the stars again, distant, indifferent, and splendid.

We take up our trek again.

Soon after, we hear cries behind us, still far away. The Enemy is about to catch up with us and we do not even know if we are close to the right road.

We are confused, troubled, frightened. We still trudge onward, like blind men, driven only by the hope of being somewhere near the right road.

A few others and I instinctively offer to stop and slow down the Enemy. We are afraid, but we are truly prepared to do it.

Vadusfadam catches up to us and points to something in the distance, under the light of the almost full moon. It seems to be a dune like all the others. No, it is more sharp-edged. We desperately run in that direction, sinking into the sand.

The spot indicated disappears every time we fall down, roll down a dune. Then it reappears nearer to the next dune on the horizon.

Cries behind us, then several black shadows rush in our direction. We turn around to face them. Our hearts, beating like mad, are in our mouths.

Vadusfadam is with us. Quickly, he tells us what position to take in order to avoid being surrounded. He stands with his feet wide apart, bends his knees a little, and grasps his walking stick with both hands. Those of us who have one, copy him.

The dark shadows, seeing our resoluteness, seem to hesitate. Then the Monk yells and rushes at them.

I feel a gigantic charge building up inside of me, a clear and terrible determination. I cry out and throw myself at the Enemy.

One of the shadows is in front of me. I can smell its stench, and I can hear it panting with a long, unpleasant hiss. I want to hit the Enemy. I have not come this far only to surrender without a fight. I deal a blow, but the shadow backs away avoiding it.

Now, we can see that our Enemies are only the van-guard of the Dark Forces that were following us before we passed through the first three Scarlet Doors. Gratefully, they are now fewer in number than our group.

This cheers us up, and we hurl ourselves forward again. Meanwhile the Monk has struck and knocked down his adversary.

We push forward again, decisively. Our Enemies hesitate, then they turn and flee.

We shout for joy!

Vadusfadam has us rejoin our group and run on ahead. He says they will return, next time in much larger numbers. But now we surely have a few hours of respite ...

In less than half an hour, we reach the hillock.

Behind it rises a strange form: Four rather tall obelisks made of red granite are set an equal distance apart and are leaning so that their summits support one another. In short, they form a pyramid, making up its corners.

That is the Fourth Scarlet Door.

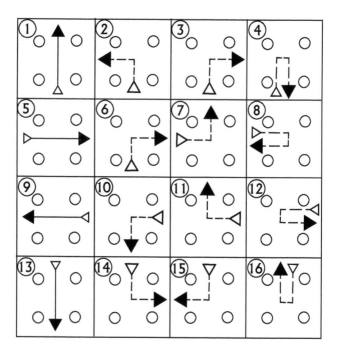

The test is to determine which pair of arches to pass under to enter the pyramid, and also which to exit.

There are sixteen ways to accomplish this task, but we must choose the path that correlates to our past lives, our karmic record. Without memory, we will only have a one in sixteen chance of success.

Each Initiate takes a turn, first recapturing the essence of their soul's prior life experience, and then selecting which path into and out of the pyramid relates to their karmic history.

It is a synchronic, intimate mystery that we all are able to pass through the Fourth Scarlet Door.

Our minds have been torn apart and reassembled, cleaned and put back together as good as new.

How many personalities I was carrying around! And all those "selves" of mine wanted to be the only "me." It was difficult creating order among the various personalities, but you can always come by help ...

You, Dear Reader: Do you need help?

Would you like a clue to help you decide which path will gain you access through the Fourth Scarlet Door?

Once again, record the time here _____. Then add together the number relative to the minute of reading this, and that relative to the hour using twenty-four hour increments (e.g., 11:00 am is 11; 11:00 pm is 23).

If the number equals or is less than 5:
>In a past life: The sea was your home.
>In this life: What you need is TRUST in others.
>Tarot Card: MAGICIAN.
>Choose passage 1.

If the number is between 6 and 10 inclusive:
>In a past life: You were a stone mason of great buildings.
>In this life: You need MEASURE and BALANCE in all things.
>Tarot Card: HIGH PRIESTESS.
>Choose passage 2.

If the number is between 11 and 15 inclusive:
>In a past life: You fished but were afraid of the water.
>In this life: You need CALM to be LESS IMPULSIVE. Count to 10 before losing your temper.
>Tarot Card: EMPRESS.
>Choose passage 3.

If the number is between 16 and 20 inclusive:
>In a past life: You led animals along difficult trails.
>In this life: Instead of letting others guide you, be more DECISIVE.
>Tarot Card: EMPEROR.
>Choose passage 4.

If the number is between 21 and 25 inclusive:
>In a past life: You died as a small child.
>In this life: You lack PLAYFULNESS, the real sort. Continue to act, but take things less seriously.
>Tarot Card: HIEROPHANT.
>Choose passage 5.

If the number is between 26 and 30 inclusive:
In a past life: Around 1650, you died of the plague, probably in Europe. You used to be a trader; your birthmarks and moles are an indication.
In this life: You need more SELF-CONFIDENCE.
Tarot Card: LOVERS.
Choose passage 6.

If the number is between 31 and 35 inclusive:
In a past life: You denounced and were denounced. You paid the price.
In this life: SINCERITY and SELF ESTEEM are vital to you.
Tarot Card: CHARIOT.
Choose passage 7.

If the number is between 36 and 42 inclusive:
In a past life: You were at one with the Gods, then you sinned and forgot.
In this life: You must learn to PRAY, to be LESS RATIONAL, and to wear fewer masks.
Tarot Card: JUSTICE.
Choose passage 8.

If the number is between 43 and 47 inclusive:
In a past life: You cultivated the land or you were a hunter and gatherer.
In this life: You follow your positive INTUITION, but you need to be LESS SUSPICIOUS of others.
Tarot Card: HERMIT.
Choose passage 9.

If the number is between 48 and 52 inclusive:
In a past life: You were a weaver. You died in childbirth.
In this life: IDEALISM is the key.
Tarot Card: STRENGTH.
Choose passage 10.

If the number is between 53 and 57 inclusive:
In a past life: You lived in the midst of wars and you were caught up in the violence, twice over.
In this life: You need COURAGE.
Tarot Card: HANGMAN.
Choose Passage 11.

If the number is between 58 and 62 inclusive:
In a past life: Music and dance were your ancient pastimes.
In this life: ADAPTATION is essential.
Tarot Card: TEMPERANCE.
Choose Passage 12.

If the number is between 63 and 67 inclusive:
In a past life: You were a female slave in the Orient.
In this life: Ponder things carefully before you speak and talk less. Utilize RESERVE and PRUDENCE.
Tarot Card: STAR.
Choose Passage 13.

If the number is between 68 and 72 inclusive:
In a past life: You plotted and fought for your people. Torture and an enclosed place killed you.
In this life: The key is IMAGINATION that goes beyond appearances.
Tarot Card: MOON.
Choose Passage 14.

If the number is between 73 and 78 inclusive:
In a past life: Riches clouded your mind and your heart was hard.
In this life: If you want to journey beyond the Fourth Scarlet Door, you must GIVE OF YOURSELF. Think about this on your own.
Tarot Card: SUN.
Choose Passage 15.

If the number is between 78 and 83 inclusive:
In a past life: You used to read, study. You were a scribe.
In this life: CREATIVE IMAGINATION is the key to your talents.
Tarot Card: JUDGEMENT.
Choose Passage 16.

Vadusfadam teaches that each of us, ultimately, will achieve perfect happiness, fulfillment, and the right road to ecstasy.

Thus, the Game of Life ends, ultimately, with total union.

But not before passing through the three remaining Scarlet Doors ...

PART FIVE
The Fifth Scarlet Door

The moon sets and dawn comes. We eat what we have found nearby; it is not much. No fire warms us. But at least we have found the road again.

We set off.

The path across the desert is straight ahead once more. It goes on forever, until, when the sun is already high, the path begins to descend in a steady slope, not so noticeable as to be steep, but enough to check our steps.

By the sides of the road the dunes are getting higher and higher until they become a gully that, as time goes by, becomes narrower and narrower. As we go on, it is getting ever more difficult to walk side by side, even just in twos.

Now the road consists of a winding path that seems to keep sinking into the ground.

The light is scarce, since we are constantly in the shade.

I think the sun can be seen for only a few minutes here each day, when it is exactly overhead. Time moves slowly.

We feel intimidated by this strange land. It seems the descent downhill never stops ...

Now the road is moving underground! We are in a tunnel with walls that are lit at equal intervals by white candles. We waver, almost imperceptibly, before moving any further forward.

We then go down and down and down.

The stone passage widens, just a little, alongside the path. The vault of the tunnel is gradually getting higher. The candles mark the way and their light merges into the boundlessness before us.

Yet, we do not see anyone changing the burned-down candles. Quite simply, as soon as they go out, an entirely fresh candle immediately appears!

Vadusfadam informs us that these lights come from faraway places on our earth, where these very same candles are kept alight in special, sacred, magical temples. They are the large wax candles that witness the rites of Humankind.

Should they ever go out or never be used again on earth, the magical candles would burn away, just like normal ones, and our underground road would be left in darkness, so that no traveler would ever again succeed in crossing this stretch to the next Door.

We ask our guide what he can tell us about the Fifth Scarlet Door.

He tells us that it has to do with transmutation – being refined through the stages of alchemy. Then, after drawing some symbols on the wall, Vadusfadam recites these words:

Alchemical Scarlet Door, Fifth of the Line:

*My Queen: I desire with interest and positive will,
from now on, the Shining City.
I shall bring leaves of gold as gifts, oh Cleopatra:
electrum, iron plate, red copper, aqua vitae, beeswax.
I shall coagulate all, I shall make crystals,
I shall filter and I shall fix.
When it is all purified, I will sublimate everything,
and again I shall purify.
I shall extract sulphur and alchemical sulphur,
in the name of the Four Elements.
All of it in the right year, month, night, and hour.*

We look at one another. We have understood very little of these words. However, we move forward, unperturbed.

We trust in the knowledge earned along this stretch of road. We overwhelm Vadusfadam with questions, conjectures, theories, intuitions.

A little at a time, we begin to draw conclusions from the initial confusion. So many tiny pieces slide into place, like in a complex puzzle.

The corridor has widened a great deal, in height and in breadth. The sound of our footsteps creates odd echoes, strange reverberations.

Meanwhile, the color of the candles has changed to green. Long shadows dance on the walls, flickering with the movement of the air caused by our passing.

These candles remind me of other fires, other moments of my life: camping sites, fireplaces, barbeques, torches, fireworks, other candles ...

I realize with a little surprise how often the experiences of each one of us are accompanied by fire.

Now, wide niches alternate with the candles lighting our way. In the niches are placed alembics, retorts, jars, pelicans, bottles, mortars, and dozens of other shapes that I am unable to identify.

The Monk toys with a die. As he walks at our side, he lets it fall three times.
The first time the number appearing face up is TWO.
The second is ONE.
The third is THREE.
He shakes the die for a fourth time but does not throw it down.[4] Instead, he smiles and looks at the candles, which have changed color once more. Now the candles are red. I imagine it means we are close to our latest goal.
Much time has passed in this underground tunnel and I am hungry. My head is going dizzy with weakness, and the back of my neck really hurts. I feel sick, aching all over. I can see that the others are feeling no better than I.
But I find the strength to put up with it. I grit my teeth and move on.

Suddenly, Vadusfadam stops us. The walls of the tunnel are veering apart. It is now a large, very long cave. The candles still go on forever.
Next to a wall, by the light of a nearby candle, the Monk draws an image on the ground. He asks us to go over it with our little fingers but without spoiling the lines so that everyone can trace it. He also tells us to fill our minds with the color red.

---

[4] Divination with dice is a reference to *The Book of Synchronicity*, written by Oberto Airaudi and available on Amazon and as an iPad app. The book operates as an Oracle, consulted by throwing a die four times in a row. The reader is invited to throw a fourth die and research the result.

For me, just looking at the image has the effect of evoking a great heat low in my belly.

I keep my left hand closed in a fist with my little finger extended. I start tracing the design. What a strange game ...

A tingling shoots through me. I go over the lines many times, over and over again. It feels as if so many things slide into place, a place that had always been there, ready for this.

This exercise awakens many powers in us, powers that we have never used before.

You too, Dear Reader:

If you wish, trace this symbol, which encapsulates your hidden talent and directs you to the Fifth Scarlet Door.

Start wherever you like, but do not remove your finger until you have finished. During this ritual, breathe deeply, regularly, in silence.

If it does not have an immediate effect on you, then try again. Use the little finger of your left hand or, ideally, a gold and silver selfic pen.[5]

Thereafter, you will dream or understand something new; otherwise, you will re-read this book more than once …

Alas, who knows where your precise road leads?

We are in front of that which the Master calls the Fifth Scarlet Door.

In a huge cavern with eight very tall white columns towering above us, there is a small opening in the wall that is lit by a triangle made of sixty-six red candles.

That is the passageway.

Vadusfadam has us immerse ourselves in a nearby well of warm water, after we have taken off all our clothes.

When I go to get dressed again, the Monk shakes his head not to, then he points in the direction of the passage.

I understand: For this test, I cannot even hang on to my clothes. I'm not even embarrassed in front of my companions. I've got other things to think about. So I shrug, then nod in agreement and set off …

---

[5] Selfica is a discipline which creates structures based on the spiral and the use of metals, colors, inks, and minerals that are able to convey intelligent energies. A selfic pen made of gold and silver is a special instrument used to trace patterns and magical signs.

My God, my God!

By the Gods, Lords of Time and Space: I have made it through!

I watched the whole of this life go by, instant by instant, as if I were about to die. I intuited with profound certainty truths that I did not know a second beforehand. I sensed the exact moment – the only moment – that I would be able to pass through the central part of the Door.

This has been the most overwhelming experience of my existences ... and recently there has been no shortage of surprises!

Who knows how much time has gone by while we were underground?

We are only just beginning to feel better. I can tell from the increase in our appetite. There is no lack of water in these caverns, but we haven't seen any food.

I count my travelling companions. Two are not with us anymore. As far as I remember, they were the ones who didn't have much to do with the other Initiates, who kept to themselves most of the time.

We ask the Time Monk what happens to those who do not manage to pass through the Fifth Scarlet Door.

He says they are sent back to the starting point and lose all memory of what happened. They also lose the chance, in the current life, of returning to the Central Fires through the Seven Scarlet Doors.

We go on a little further.

Vadusfadam does not let us slow down. He reminds us that the Enemies we put to flight are looking for us, determined to destroy us. He tells us that as we progress, we become more precious in the Game of Life, and therefore more dangerous to the Anti-Evolutionary Forces.

Eventually, fatigue weighs upon everyone. Even Vadusfadam seems worn out. He has been there for us, at our side, and he has not complained once. How much patience he must have to accept us as we are.

I pass close to him. He looks at me and then stops me. Gently taking my arm, he says, "I guide you because I love you." Then he releases me and moves on ahead.

Can he read our thoughts? Did he sense what I was thinking? Why is he there with a reply some times, and at other times he pretends not to have heard, even when asked directly for help?

We have reached a circular cave, much smaller than the one where we found the Fifth Door. In the center, a lovely, crackling fire awaits us, and there are blankets, some clean tunics in all sizes, and food.

I've got my appetite back all of a sudden. But Vadusfadam hastens to remind us that after fasting for days, it is well to eat very little for now and mainly take liquids.

It is hard to restrain ourselves, but all of us follow his advice ... except one. That Initiate will be ill later on, and he will be sent back to the starting point, with no memory of these amazing experiences.

So even that was a test!

We eat like convalescents. We sleep. We wake up and eat again. We chat a lot among ourselves. Some play with the echoes in the cavern.

Then we start on our way again.

Around us, we notice dozens and dozens of other caves. Some are dark; others are lit by different colored candles: black candles, white candles, green ones, candles made from dung, others of yellow or pure brown beeswax.

The Time Monk advises us to keep on following the red candles, which soon take us on a winding course. We are in an underground labyrinth. Finally, the road straightens out, to our great relief.

Suddenly, all the red candles – spanning the entire length of the long passage we are moving through – flicker and go out. We freeze in the total darkness. We can distinctly hear our own breathing.

Vadusfadam whispers that someone up there, above ground in our world, has let a sacred candle go out without replacing it.

We stand mostly still, groping blindly for each other with our hands. I do not know how long the darkness lasts, but we are beginning to feel anxious.

And now we hear frightening sounds coming from an adjoining corridor, echoing throughout the tunnel! It is our Enemies looking for us ...

Dear Reader:

If you want to help your friends who are being chased in an unlit underground cave, offer a small red candle to the Gods. Then pick up the book again when the candle has burned out, or at some other time.

Truly, it isn't good to read this book all in one go. If you want to train your will, turn back to the poem in this section that Vadusfadam recited and re-read everything up to here again.

However, if you cannot resist carrying on, or if you find this book to be nothing more than a peculiar entertaining text, then by all means proceed ...

Part Six
The Sixth Scarlet Door

So let us go on, now that you have made up your mind and have acted of your free will.

Suddenly the candles along our path have lit up again. Someone up there loves us! We try to make up for lost time and find a good hiding place.

Carefully, silently, Vadusfadam leads us through the labyrinth. We go on for a very long time, but none of us complains.

Twice more we catch a glimpse of the Enemy shadows looking for us. I believe that something in us has changed. Since passing beyond the Fifth Door, it seems more difficult for the Enemy to identify us.

The Time Monk confirms this impression of ours.

We go on for a long way still. Then I become aware that the road is meandering slightly uphill. Perhaps we are coming back up to the surface!

So we are.

Much, much later we find ourselves in a wide space surrounded by steep walls of rock. But I can see the sky – we are out in the open!

We notice, however, that we cannot see the rest of the road; it appears to stop here.

We wonder if we have arrived at a Central Fire? Yet, we don't see a fire of any kind.

Vadusfadam tells us that we were in the caves for three days, but no more information is forthcoming.

The sun must have only just gone down, since it is becoming dark. Now, before nightfall, it is up to us to find some wood and light a good fire.

There are wild roots here, fruit, flowers, animals to hunt. We have to find food and warmth by the efforts of our own hands.

I make a bow, using the belt from the tunic I am wearing. Some gather wood for the fire. Others look for fruit and wild roots. We have discovered that we now can recognize what is edible from what is not.

The Fifth Scarlet Door has given us knowledge and powers that come to the surface when we need them, and not a moment before.

As we wander around preparing the fire and our meal, the Time Monk tells us to pick up the first stone that appeals to us, however big or small, and carry it with us on this next stage of our journey.

You too, Dear Reader:

If you want to face the Sixth Door, you must go out of the house, look for, and for a whole day take everywhere with you the first stone that appeals to you, large or small.

RIDICULOUS

All this is ridiculous, you may say.

Well then, take a good look within. Are you so hung up on the notion that others might say something to you, make fun of you, that you cannot even summon up the courage to take a stone from the ground and put it in your pocket?

Or will you keep your stone well hidden so you don't have to explain it? Will you put it on your desk where no one else will see it?

If so, never mind. Close this book. It is not for you. Continue to make all the excuses in the world for yourself. After all, my dear friend, isn't that what you've always done up to now? Think about it …

Free yourself. It is high time! Give vent to your imagination and don't give in to your fears! Prove to yourself how free, independent, and detached you are. Measure just how far your shame, your dread of ridicule, your fear of others extends. Prove to yourself, beyond a doubt, what you believe to be "civilized" limits.

Go on then ... go outside and find a little, innocent stone. And while you search for the right stone, have a think.

This book knows how to wait for you.

All well and good. Here we are again.

I will say nothing more on our previous topic. I will let it rest. The facts speak for themselves.

Vadusfadam is sitting on the ground. He wants us to meditate on our stones.

We gather around the fire. Everyone looks at their stone, passing it from one hand to the other.

He says to us, "It is a true, silent friend who will never betray you. It doesn't talk, yet stays with you, listening to you for as long as you want. And if you throw it away, it won't protest. It won't complain even if you are ashamed of it."

Then the Monk falls silent.

High above us is the full moon.

We wonder, privately, how this exercise will help us pass through the Sixth Scarlet Door.

Suddenly, magically, Vadusfadam is surrounded by myriads of musical instruments. He tells us that in order to pass through the Sixth Door, we must first learn to play at least one instrument, every one of us. Only then will we be able to pass through it.

We get on with it, and after we have eaten we play, we experiment, swapping instruments every now and then. We put everything into it. We discover that the Fifth Door has enabled us to develop surprising musical and rhythmical talents.

Vadusfadam gets to his feet and recites these verses relating to the Sixth Scarlet Door:

Cymbals, shells, trumpets, drums clap their hands.
Songs, stamping, moos and baas, cries,
laughter of children and adults.
Fear, adventure, sense of disappearance,
excitement, courage, prayers.
Low and profound vibrations,
the glasses tremble and the columns.

One step ahead, the tail, I wait for another step.
There are always less of us to sing, they pass and disappear,
pulling the calf beyond the threshold.
How can we catch the rabbits if they are not asleep?
Self, no other metal, now it's my turn.
I keep silent, I now have my mouth full of seeds.
I hold my breath, jump …

We remember the dance steps that we learned at the start of the journey. We begin reciting, singing, and playing as we discover new powers, rhythms, abilities within us.

Clapping the stones together makes a sharp reverberating noise, bouncing off the rock walls. The sound takes us, resounds through us, becomes part of us.

The moon is still high above us.

After a little while, the Monk stands up and we set off again, illuminated by the light of the celestial body.

He accompanies us to a path hidden by bushes, high up. I hear an "Oh!" of amazement. Beyond those branches is a wide-curved stretch of pebble beach and lively sea, full of character and strength. Strange that we didn't pick up the scent of sea spray! But what isn't strange on this journey?

We light another fire on the beach. Then Vadusfadam makes us build a pyre where the waves and the land meet. We go bring some large stones, positioning them where the waves ebb. We run away, laughing, as the waves rush in toward us.

We play with the sea for a long time. It steals our stones and moves them, but in the end we construct a wide, dry base, as tall as we stand and shaped like the sides of a pyramid.

We place branches and logs brought from the sea on top to shelter the newly lit fire from excessive draughts. We add dry canes, sea weed, some more branches and withered thicket.

The flames blaze high. Red and yellow sparks rise up into the sky in a bright column. We are moved, without quite knowing why.

Sea, we offer you this fire; fire, we dedicate this sea to you. And may you be happy and wedded to one another.

Small and great stars and you – oh, witnessing moon, silent veiled lady – bathe us in your magic light!

I sense something ancient inside of me. Something that has always been hidden without my realizing it, something that now is growing and awakening at last ...

With his long stick, Vadusfadam has drawn large spirals in the sand and between the rocks. We lay down some stones to mark out the lines. Complex, strange patterns drawn under the moon – a complicated path to the fire over the sea.

We sing, we dance. The night lasts forever. The moon has shifted slightly, in the direction of the pyre and toward the water.

We keep on playing, singing. Energies fostered by the elements ignite within us. Then the Time Monk makes us walk around the spiraling lines several times. Each time, a vision emerges of a spiritually advanced community, growing, expanding.

The moon sets. Soon it will skim the sea behind the pyre, on which the fire still blazes high.

We can sense it: The moment has come and we line up in silence. One at a time, Vadusfadam has us run toward the pyre, climb on top of it, and throw ourselves through the fire and off to the other side.

Like parachutists in a line, we hurl ourselves up and over the fire one at a time. My heart is beating hard. Just two more and then it is my turn ...

Sudden shouts and screeches at our backs! Dozens of black figures are running toward us from the far side of the beach. More of them are coming, ever so many. It is the Enemy, and they want to stop us from completing this rite, at all costs.

Vadusfadam tells us to keep on going.

Scores and scores of frantic thoughts go through my mind. I have always been afraid of death, now more than ever. I have tried to hide it from myself and to block it out, but it has always been there, waiting inside of me: fear for my safety, fear of pain, of losing my physical well being.

I have tried everything during my life to suppress this fear of death, but it has always been with me. By fearing it, I know I invoke it at times.

I have a hidden terror of finding signs of decline when I awaken each morning, perhaps a swelling, a strange pain.

And I fear becoming ill, so much so that I would swallow anything in order to keep my health.

I have seen animals grow old and die, people dear to me pass from life to stillness. I even wished, when I was a child, that it would never touch me ...

Now that the Enemy is coming and I stand still waiting for it, I am completely terrified of dying, of being hurt.

But I also desire to go on – I will not flee! One more Initiate left. And then it is my turn to go along the spiral track toward the fire.

But our Enemies are almost here ...

Now!

Breathing hard, I take off at a run. I see the altar becoming larger and larger before me. Here it is.

I climb up. I jump through the fire and over it ...

Beyond those red flames – between sky, fire, earth and sea – I feel suspended, stopped in time. A thousand knots loosen in me, a thousand pieces fall into place.

I feel ripped open.

I laugh and cry with happiness, with joy. I am being born right now, as a New Human ...

I am in the sea.

Above me, it is daylight. Behind me, the pyre no longer exists. There is only a tropical island with very fine white sand.

I walk on the seabed, between fishes that are hardly disturbed by my presence.

And I join those Initiates who arrived ahead of me.

Part Seven
The Seventh Scarlet Door

Meanwhile, the rest of my companions appear like a shot from nowhere. All of them! We all made it through the Sixth Door!

Lastly, Vadasfadam appears, though bleeding on the forehead and from one hand.

This place is wonderful, stunningly beautiful.

We gather on the beach around the Monk and bind his wounds.

He says, "Now, all you have to do is build a City of Light, form your own nation, a civilization that opens up the way for others. This is the most effective way to beat the Enemy. Then, you will pass beyond the Seventh Door."

The Seventh Scarlet Door!

"Where is it, Master?" we ask.

"Here, can you not see it?"

I turn around, then around again. I take a good look ... and I begin to understand. And to see it clearly.

"I want to go, Master. With you," I emphasize. "I love you as you love us. And I understand now what our mission entails."

Without any hurry, our adventure continues. It cannot come to an end.

The Enemy will be defeated, I swear it.

And all of us – all of the aware men and women who so wish, who have the courage to be resolute – will glimpse the ultimate goal of the Game of Life offered to Humankind.

A new caravan sets off tomorrow on the path on the mountain that does not yet exist.

Are *you* coming?

The Time Monk will be with us, just as he is with YOU!

Those who see and who seek Enlightenment
play the Game of Life.

Those who do not give up
and who live
and who dare
and who know how to distinguish
conquer the Enemy.

Thus will you be led beyond
The Seven Scarlet Doors.

EPILOGUE

The Seventh Scarlet Door is the most mysterious of all ... It is a portal to our powers of Co-Creation. It is a gateway to the elevation of the Collective Conciousness.

Thanks to our guides – Time Monks OroCritshna and Vadusfadam – the road to the Central Fires is now accessible from anywhere in the world.

And the number of Initiates is growing!

For me and my companions, our journey continues.

We must stay alert, as the road is not marked beyond this beach. And we must travel it together, looking for and sharing the synchronous clues that lead us toward a new and glorious destiny ...

Vadusfadam has left our Community, but every now and again he returns with a new group of Initiates.

We are excited when he visits, and we celebrate with food and drink, music and dance.

His last instructions to us were as follows:

You will manifest a City of Light only when you have reached the exact number of brothers and sisters for that purpose. They will arrive from all times and naturally gather together after remembering their prior lives and their current roles.

Such Cities of Light will form as long as time provides. But know that there is a time duration to the Game of Life and that the Enemy does not rest.

These are beautiful days: intense, tiring, and full.

Everyone has learned to play their own instrument, constantly acquiring new skills, new knowledge.

We manage on our own now.

We cultivate the land to feed ourselves. We have learned to weave. We find practically everything we need in this strange land.

And providence is always with us, as there are occasions when we gratefully receive help. It is an indication that the path we are following is correct, at least I hope that is so and so I believe.

So much joy inside of me! So many things to do!

New territories frequently surface – so many that we do not have time to explore them all.

We stay together as our numbers grow. And the latest arrivals quickly acclimate to the pace.

Building houses. Farming. Making our clothes.

There also are myriads of things we could manage without, but which represent the exercise books in which we do our "homework."

And the Time Monk corrects them all, with care.

In short, we New Humans are getting on with building it: *the first City of Light.*

It represents the Seventh Scarlet Door, and the birth of a new civilization of Enlightened Human Beings.

Thus, may each of YOU become an Initiate.

And join us in laying a new stretch of road so that others may find the Central Fires.

ABOUT THE AUTHOR

OBERTO *"Falco"* AIRAUDI

Oberto Airaudi is Damanhur's Spiritual Guide. His teachings encourage the awakening of the inner master through study, experimentation, overcoming dogmatic attitudes, and the complete expression of individual potential.

Born in 1950 in Balangero, Italy (near Turin), Mr. Airaudi is a philosopher, healer, writer, and painter. He is constantly involved in research into cutting-edge therapeutic applications, the arts and new sciences. In accordance with the Damanhurian custom of being called by animal names, Mr. Airaudi also uses the name of "Falco" (Falcon).

He chose this name to honor Horus, symbol of the divine principle to be awakened inside every human being and the cosmic God of the New Millennium.

From a very early age, Falco manifested a clear spiritual vision and the gift of healing. He committed to develop these gifts through constant and exacting experimentation, outside of traditional academic institutions. His spiritual and personal growth continued over the years via incessant studies, journeys of research, the awakening of his memories, the development of artistic skills, and the rediscovery of ancient knowledge.

In 1975, Falco founded the Horus Center in Turin. It was the first seed of a Mystery School and a community, and from its activities the Federation of Damanhur developed.

Damanhur was born to realize the dream of a society based on optimism and the idea that human beings can be the masters of their own destiny, without having to depend on other forces outside themselves. Indeed, the basis of Falco's vision is the belief that every human being participates, through conscious interactions with others, to awaken a divine nature within themselves. As a result, Damanhur is a society in constant evolution and transformation, based on the exaltation of diversity. Its social, political, and philosophical systems are always in flux.

Falco is a remarkably reserved person, and he has no decision-making role within the political or social structure of Damanhur, which is directed by elected bodies. If asked, he is always available to cooperate with the Federation's Guides, who are elected by the citizens.

ABOUT DAMANHUR

Founded in 1975, the Federation of Damanhur is an Italian eco-society based upon ethical and spiritual values. Damanhur has about 1,000 citizens and extends over 500 hectares of land throughout the Valchiusella region, at the foothills of the Piedmont Alps.

Damanhur is approximately 90% self-sustainable, with more than 80 businesses that foster agricultural and economic independence. Damanhur has a Constitution, complementary currency system, daily newspaper, art studios, centers for research and practice of medicine and science, open university, and education for children from elementary through middle school.

Damanhur promotes a culture of peace and equitable development through solidarity, volunteerism, respect for the environment, art, and social and political engagements. Courses and events are open to the public year round, and it is possible to visit for short periods as well as longer stays for study, vacation, or regeneration.

Damanhur's Temples of Humankind – often called the "Eighth Wonder of the World" – comprise an extraordinary underground network of chapels dedicated to the reawakening of the divine essence in every human being. The art studios that contributed to the stained glass, mosaics, and frescoes in the Temples are located at Damanhur Crea, a center for innovation, wellness, and research, which is open to the public every day of the year.

Damanhur operates additional centers in Italy, Europe, Japan, and the United States. Damanhur also collaborates with other international organizations engaged in the social, civic, and spiritual development of the planet.

Damanhur has received world-wide recognition for its innovative and inspiring approach to life. Since 1988, Damanhur has been a member of the Global Eco-Villages Network, and in 2005 it received a United Nations sustainability award. In 2007, *EnlightenNext* magazine voted Damanhur the most evolved community on earth.

Please visit the Damanhur website for additional information and directions on how to visit the community.

www.Damanhur.org

ABOUT THE PUBLISHER

The Truth

The founders of The Oracle Institute are gravely concerned that the greatest crisis facing humanity is the resurgence of religious intolerance perpetrated in the name of God. We chose the Pentacle as our icon because, to us, this symbol represents the emerging spiritual unification of the five primary religions: Hinduism, Judaism, Buddhism, Christianity, and Islam. We believe the time has come for humanity to shed archaic belief systems and prepare for the next phase of our collective spiritual evolution.

The Love

The Oracle Institute promotes a process of soul growth which includes study, worship, meditation, and good works through application of the Golden Rule: the "Eleventh Commandment" brought by Jesus. When we earnestly strive to perfect ourselves, practice compassion toward others, and assume responsibility for the health of our planet, we help birth a new spiritual paradigm.

The Light

Many people are now ready to manifest "heaven on earth" – the prophesied era of abundance, peace, and harmony foretold by the prophets of every religion and the elders of every indigenous wisdom culture. To that end, The Oracle Institute offers interfaith books, spirituality classes, civics seminars, health and mindfulness programs, and holistic products designed to foster the quest for spiritual enlightenment.

We Invite You to Join Us on Our Journey of

TRUTH, LOVE, and LIGHT

Donations may be made to:

THE ORACLE INSTITUTE
A 501(c)(3) Educational Charity

*An Advocate for Enlightenment and
A Vanguard for Spiritual Evolution*

1990 Battlefield Drive
Independence, Virginia 24348
www.TheOracleInstitute.org

All donations and proceeds from our books and classes are used to further our educational mission and to build the Peace Pentagon, an interfaith and social justice center in Independence, Virginia.

Lightning Source UK Ltd.
Milton Keynes UK
UKHW020717241221
396151UK00009B/2077